Allan Ramsay

The Ever Green - A Collection of Scots Poems

Volume First

Allan Ramsay

The Ever Green - A Collection of Scots Poems
Volume First

ISBN/EAN: 9783744716017

Printed in Europe, USA, Canada, Australia, Japan

Cover: Foto ©Andreas Hilbeck / pixelio.de

More available books at **www.hansebooks.com**

The Ever Green

A COLLECTION

OF

Scots Poems

Wrote by the Ingenious before 1600

By ALLAN RAMSAY

Reprinted from the Original Edition

IN TWO VOLUMES

VOLUME FIRST

Glasgow

ROBERT FORRESTER, 1 ROYAL EXCHANGE SQUARE

1876

Printed by M'LAREN & ERSKINE, *Glasgow.*

THE
Ever Green,

BEING A

COLLECTION
OF
SCOTS POEMS,

Wrote by the Ingenious before 1600.

VOL. I.

Publiſhed by ALLAN RAMSAY.

Still green with Bays each ancient Altar ſtands,
Above the Reach of ſacrilegious Hands,
Secure from Flames, from Envys fiercer Rage,
Deſtructive War and all devouring Age.
             POPE.

EDINBURGH,
Printed by Mr. THOMAS RUDDIMAN for the Pu-
bliſher, at his Shop, near the Croſs. M.DCC.XXIV.

To His GRACE

JAMES

Duke of HAMILTON, &c.

Captain General,

And the reſt of the Honourable
MEMBERS of the

Royal COMPANY *of* ARCHERS.

My LORDS *and* GENTLEMEN,

WHEN the more eminent Concerns
of Life, or the agreeable Diver-
ſion of the BOW, do not employ your
leaſure

leaſure Time, the following OLD BARDS preſent you with an Intertainment that can never be diſagreeable to any SCOTS Man, who deſpiſes the Fopery of admiring nothing but what is either new or foreign, and is a Lover of his Country. Such the Royal Company of ARCHERS are, and ſuch every good Man ſhould ſtrive to be.

THE Spirit of Freedom that ſhines throw both the ſerious and comick Performances of our old Poets, appears of a Piece with that Love of Liberty that our antient Heroes contended for, and maintained Sword in Hand. From you then, *My Lords and Gentlemen,* who take Pleaſure to repreſent our brave Anceſtors, theſe POETS claim Regard and Patronage ; they now make a Demand for that Immortal

Fame

Fame that tuned their Souls some Hundred Years ago, which is in your Power, by countenancing to beftow. They do not addrefs you with an indigent Face, and a Thousand pityful Apologies, to bribe the good Will of the Criticks. No! 'tis long fince they were fuperiour to the Spleen of thefe four Gentlemen.

Every one who has Generofity, and is not byaffed with a miftaken Prejudice, will allow, that good Senfe, fharp Satyre, and witty Mirth, may be exprefs'd with a true Spirit, altho' in antiquated Words and Phrafes: When one beftows but a very fmall Pains to enter into the Authors Manner, then 'tis not to be doubted but the Royal Company will receive and approve of thefe valuable Remains, and have a due Regard to the Memory of thefe

thefe meritorious Authors, and accept this
Dedication from,

My Lords *and* Gentlemen,

Their faithful Publifher,

And your moft humble

And devoted Servant,

Allan Ramsay.

Edin. Octob.
15. 1724.

PREFACE.

I *Have obferved that* Readers *of the beft and moft exquifite Difcernment frequently complain of our* modern Writings, *as filled with affe&ed Delicacies and ftudied Refinements, which they would gladly exchange for that natural Strength of Thought and Simplicity of Stile our Forefathers pra&ifed:* To fuch, *I hope, the following* Colle&ion of Poems *will not be difpleafing.*

When thefe good old Bards *wrote, we had not yet made Ufe of imported* Trimming *upon our* Cloaths, *nor of foreign* Embroidery *in our* Writings. *Their* Poetry *is the* Produ& *of their own* Country, *not pilfered and fpoiled in the* Tranfportation *from abroad:* Their Images *are native, and their* Landfkips *domef-*

tick

tick; copied from thoſe Fields and Meadows we every Day behold.

The Morning *riſes (in the Poets Deſcription) as ſhe does in the* Scottiſh *Horizon. We are not carried to* Greece *or* Italy *for a Shade, a Stream or a Breeze.* The Groves *riſe in our own Valleys; the* Rivers *flow from our own Fountains, and the* Winds *blow upon our own Hills. I find not Fault with thoſe Things, as they are in* Greece *or* Italy : *But with a* North-ern Poet *for fetching his Materials from theſe Places, in a Poem, of which his own Country is the Scene; as our* Hymners *to the* Spring *and* Makers *of* Paſ-torals *frequently do.*

This Miſcellany *will likewiſe recommend itſelf, by the Diverſity of Subjects and Humour it contains.* The grave Deſcription *and the wanton* Story, *the* Moral Saying *and the mirthful* Jeſt, *will illuſtrate and alternately relieve each other.*

The Reader *whoſe Temper is ſpleen'd with the* Vices *and* Follies *now in* Faſhion, *may gratifie his Humour with the* Satyres *he will here find upon the* Follies *and* Vices *that were uppermoſt two or three*

Hun-

Hundred Years ago. The Man, whose Inclinations are turned to Mirth, *will be pleased to know how the good Fellow of a former Age told his jovial Tale; and the* Lover *may divert himself with the old fashioned Sonnet of an amorous Poet in* Q. Margaret *and* Q. Mary's Days. *In a Word, the following* Collection *will be such another Prospect to the Eye of the Mind, as to the outward Eye is the various Meadow, where Flowers of different Hue and Smell are mingled together in a beautiful Irregularity.*

I hope also the Reader, *when he dips into these* Poems, *will not be displeased with this Reflection, That he is stepping back into the Times that are past, and that exist no more. Thus the* Manners *and* Customs *then in Vogue, as he will find them here described, will have all the Air and Charm of* Novelty; *and that seldom fails of exciting Attention and pleasing the Mind. Besides, the* Numbers, *in which these* Images *are conveyed, as they are not now commonly practised, will appear new and amusing.*

The different Stanza and varied Cadence will likewise much sooth and engage the Ear, which in

Poetry

Poetry *especially muſt be always flattered. However, I do not expect that theſe* Poems *ſhould pleaſe every* Body, *nay the critical* Reader *muſt needs find ſeveral* Faults; *for I own that there will be found in theſe* Volumes *two or three Pieces, whoſe* Antiquity *is their greateſt Value; yet ſtill I am perſwaded there are many more that ſhall merit* Approbation *and* Applauſe *than* Cenſure *and* Blame. *The beſt Works are but a Kind of* Miſcellany, *and the cleaneſt Corn is not without ſome Chaff, no not after often Winnowing:* Beſides, Diſpraiſe *is the eaſieſt Part of* Learning, *and but at beſt the Offspring of* uncharitable Wit. *Every Clown can ſee that the Furrow is crooked, but where is the Man that will plow me one ſtraight?*

There is nothing can be heard more ſilly than one's expreſſing his Ignorance *of his* native Language; *yet ſuch there are, who can vaunt of acquiring a tolerable Perfection in the* French *or* Italian Tongues, *if they have been a Forthnight in* Paris *or a Month in* Rome: *But ſhew them the moſt elegant Thoughts in a* Scots Dreſs, *they as diſdainfully as ſtupidly con-*
demn

demn it as barbarous. But the true Reason is obvious: Every one that is born never so little superior to the Vulgar, *would fain distinguish themselves from them by some Manner or other, and such, it would appear, cannot arrive at a better* Method. *But this affected Class of Fops give no Uneasiness, not being numerous; for the most part of our* Gentlemen, *who are generally Masters of the most useful and politest* Languages, *can take Pleasure (for a Change) to speak and read their own.*

It was intended that an Account of the Authors *of the following* Collection *should be given; but not being furnished with such distinct Information as could be wished for that End at present, the* Design *is delayed, until the publishing of a* Third *or* Fourth *succeeding* Volume, *wherein the* Curious *shall be satisfied, in as far as can be gathered, with Relation to their* Lives *and* Characters, *and the Time wherein they flourished. The Names of the* Authors, *as we find them in our* Copies, *are marked before or after their* Poems.

I cannot finish this Preface, *without grateful Acknow-*

Acknowledgements to the Honourable Mr. WILLIAM CARMICHAEL, *Advocate, Brother to the Earl of* Hyndford, *who, with an easy Beneficence, that is inseparable from a superior Mind, affisted me in this* Undertaking *with a valuable Number of* Poems *in a large* Manuscript-book *in* Folio, *collected and wrote by Mr.* George Bannyntine *in Anno* 1568; *from which MS. the most of the following are gathered: And if they prove acceptable to the World, they may have the Pleasure of expecting a great many more, and shall very soon be gratified.*

CHRYSTS-

CHRYSTS-KIRK

OF THE

GRENE.

———⊹⊱•⊰⊹———

I.

WAS nevir in *Scotland* hard nor fene
    Sic Dancing and Deray,
Nowthir at *Falkland* on the Grene,
    Nor *Pebills* at the Play,

As

NOTES.

Becaufe we ftrictly obferve the old Orthography, for the more Conveniency of the Readers, we fhall note fome general Rules at the Bottom of the Page, as they occur, wherein the old Spelling differs from the prefent, in Words that have nothing elfe of the Antique, or Difference from the *Englifh*: But fhall refer you to the Gloffary at the End of the fecond Vol. for the Explanation of all of that kind in particular, and of thofe that are more peculiar to this Nation.

    Rule I. *Grene, Sene, Clene,* &c., Green, Seen, Clean. The double *ee* is fupplied in fuch Words, commonly with one *e* before, and another after the Confonant.

As was of Wowers, as I wene,
    At *Chryſts-Kirk* on a Day;
Thair came our Kitties waſhen clene
    In new Kirtills of Gray,
                Full gay,
At *Chryſt-Kirk* of the Grene that Day.

II.

To danſs thir Damyſells them dicht,
    Thir Laſſes licht of Laits:
Thair Gluvis war of the Raffell richt,
    Thair Shune war of the Straits;
Thair Kirtills war of Lincome licht,
    Weil preſt with mony Plaits:
They war ſae nyſs when Men them nicht,
    They ſqueilt lyke ony Gaits,
Sae loud, at, &c. that Day.

III. Of

Danſs, Fenſs, Glanſs, Dance, Fence, Glance.   The *ſs* us'd for the *ce* often in ſuch Words.

Dicht, Licht, Richt, &c., Dight, Light, Right.   The *ch* in ſuch Words always us'd in Place of the *gh.*

Gluvis, Luſe, Haif, &c., Gloves, Love, Have.   The *f* and *v* in-differently made uſe of in thoſe and the like Words.

Shune, Mune, Sune, &c., Shoon (or Shoes), Moon, Soon, the double *oo* never found in ſuch Words.   Sometimes they are ſpell'd, *Sone, Mone;* but in thoſe, as in many others, we have endeavour'd to fix the Orthography to the moſt frequent Manner.

III.

Of all thir Maidens myld as meid,
   Was nane fae jimp as *Gillie:*
As ony Rofe her Rude was reid,
   Her Lyre was lyke the Lillie.
Fow zellow, zellow was her Heid;
   But fcho of Lufe fae filly,
Thocht all hir Kin had fworn hir Deid,
   Scho wald haif but fweit *Willie*
Alane, at *Chryft-Kirk*, &c. that Day.

IV.

Scho fkornit *Jok* and fkrapit at him,
   And murgeont him with Mokks,
He wald haif luvit, fcho wald not lat him,
   For all his zellow Lokks.

He

Weil, Deid, Heid, Meid, &c., Well, Dead, Head, Mead. The Dipthong *ei* us'd in many fuch Words as now require *e, ea* and *ee.*

Sae, Wae, Mae, Nane, Wald, &c., So, Wo, Moe, None, Would. The *a* and *ae* in Place of *o* and *oe,* except in thofe Words, *Ony, Mony,* which are the reverfe.

Nyfs, Wyfs, Byt, Hyd, Myld, Lyk, &c., Nice, Wife, Bite, Hide, Mild, Like. Our not founding the *i* as the *Englifh* do, accounts very well for our Elders fpelling all words with a *y* of fuch a Sound.

He chereiſt hir, ſcho bad gae chat him,
　　Scho compt him not twa Clokks:
Sae ſchamefully his ſchort Goun ſet him,
　　His Limms wer lyk twa Rokks,
Scho ſaid at, &c. that Day.

V.

THOM LUTAR was thair Menſtral meit,
　　O Lord! as he could lanſs:
He playt ſae ſchill, and ſang ſae ſweet,
　　Quhyle *Towſie* tuke a Tranſs.
Auld *Lightfute* thair he did forleit,
　　And counterfittet *Franſs;*
He us'd himſelf as Man diſcreit,
　　And up tuke *Moreis* Danſs,
Full loud, at, &c. that Day.

VI.　Then

Sang, Lang, Band, Thrang, &c., Song, Long, Bond, Throng. The *a* is us'd in place of *o.*

Tuke, Blude, Gude, Luke, Fule, Shute, &c., Took, Blood, Good, Look, Fool, Shoot.

Quhyle, Quhat, Quho, Quhyt, &c., While, What, Who, White. The *qu* is always us'd for the German *w,* when an *h* immediately follows. See Mr. *Ruddiman's* Gloſſary to *Gavin Douglas's* Virgil.

Auld, Bauld, &c., Old, Bold. Here in many ſuch Words the *Scots* ſpell with *au* in Place of the *Engliſh o.*

VI.

THEN *Steven* came ftepand in with Stends,
  Nae Rynk micht him arreift:
Plateflute he bobbit up with Bends,
  For *Mald* he maid Requeift.
He lap till he lay on his Lends;
  But ryfand was fae preift,
Quhyle that he hoiftit at baith Ends,
  For honour of the Feift,
And danft, at, *&c.* that Day.

VII. SYNE

Stepand, Ryfand, &c., Stepping, Rifing; *and* is frequently the Sign of the Participle of the Prefent Tenfe; fometimes *an* and *in* inftead of the modern *ing*.

Stevin, Stepand, Stends, as before, *Laffes licht of Laits,* and generally through all, our antient Bards endeavour to add a delicate and artful Smoothnefs to their Verfe, by a Flow of Words that begin with the fame initial Letters. No Poets of any Language ever purfued that Manner fo clofe, or fucceeded fo well. *Dryden* and *Waller,* and fome others of our beft Moderns, in their Verfification, feem to admire that Beauty.

When Man on many multiply'd his Kind. Dryd.

And, *Oh! how I long my tender Limbs to lay.* Wal.

One cannot help fmiling to hear the Writer of Mr. *Waller's* Life fay, *That this Way of throwing off a Verfe eafily was firft introduced by him.*

VII.

SYNE *Robene Roy* begoud to revell,
    And *Dawny* to him druggit.
Let be, quoth *Jok*, and cawd him Jevell,
    And be the Tail him tuggit.
The Kenſie cleikit to a cavell;
    But, Lord, than how they luggit.
Thay partit manly with a Nevell;
    I trow that Hair was ruggit
Betwix them, at, &c. that Day.

VIII.

ANE bent a Bow, ſic Sturt coud ſteir him,
    Grit Skayth weſd to haif ſkard him:
He cheiſt a Flane as did affeir him;
    The toder ſaid, *Dirdum, dardum:*

Throw

Begoud, Beuk, Clam, Keiſt, &c., Began, or did begin, did bake, did climb, did caſt. Our old Authors have a great many of ſuch Preterites of Verbs, moſt of which continue amongſt us ſtill.

Toder, Fader, Bruder, Moder, Hider, &c., That other, Father, Brother, Mother, Hither. The *d* is frequently us'd for *th* in ſuch Words.

Throw baith the Cheiks he thocht to cheir him,
  Or throw the Erſs haif chard him.
Be ane Akerbraid it came not neir him,
  I can not tell quhat mard him
Thair at, *&c.* that Day.

IX.

WITH that a Freynd of his cry'd fy,
  And up an Arrow drew;
He forgit it ſae furiouſly,
  The Bow in Flenders flew:
Sae was the Will of God, trow I;
  For had the Tree been trew,
Men ſaid that kend his Archery,
  He wald haif ſlain enow
At *Chryſt-Kirk* on the Grene that Day.

X.

ANE haſty Henſure callit *Hary*,
  Quha was an Archer heynd,
Tytt up a Taikle withouten tary,
  That torment ſae him teynd.

I wat

I wat not quhidder his Hand coud vary,
 Or the Man was his Freynd;
For he eſchapit throw Michts of *Mary*,
 As Man that nae Ill meind,
But Gude, at *Chryſt-Kirk* on the Grene that Day.

XI.

THAN *Lowry* lyk a Lyon lap,
 And ſone a Flane can fedder;
He hecht to perſe him at the Pap,
 Thereon to wed a Weddir.
He hit him on the Wame a Wap,
 It buſt lyk ony Bledder:
But ſwa his Fortune was and Hap,
 His Doublet made of Ledder,
Saiſt him, at, &c. that Day.

XII.

A zaip zung Man that ſtude him neiſt,
 Louſd aff a Schot with Yre;
He ettlit the Bern in at the Breiſt,
 The Bolt flew owre the Byre,

          Ane

Zellow, Zaip, Zung, Zier, Zou, &c., Yellow, Yap, Young, Year, You.

Ane cryd, Fy, he had ſlain a Prieſt,
   A Myle bezond a Myre.
Then Bow and Bag frae him he keiſt,
   And fled as ferſs as Fyre
Frae Flint, at, *&c.* that Day.

XIII.

With Forks and Flails, thay lent grit Flaps,
   And flang togidder lyk Friggs:
With Bowgars of Barns thay beft blew Kapps,
   Quhyle thay of Berns maid Briggs.
The Reird raiſe rudely with the Rapps,
   Quhen Rungs war laid on Riggs:
The Wyfis came forth with Crys and Clapps,
   Lo, quhair my Lyking liggs,
Quoth thay, at, *&c.* that Day.

XIV.

Thay girnit and lute gird with Grains,
   Ilk Goſſip uder greivt:
Sum ſtrak with Stings, ſum gaddert Stains,
   Sum fled and ill miſchevt.

                   The

The Menſtral wan within twa Wains,
   That Day full weil he preivt:
For he came hame with unbirs'd Bains,
   Quhair Fechtairs war miſcheivt,
For evir, at, *&c.* that Day.

XV.

HEICH *Hutchon* with a Hiſſil Ryſs,
   To red can throw them rummill;
He muddillt them down lyk ony Myſs,
   He was nae Baity bummill.
Thocht he was wicht, he was nocht wyſs,
   With ſic Jangleurs to jummill;
For frae his Thoume they dang a Sklyſs,
   Quhyle he cry'd *Barlafummill,*
I am ſlain, at, *&c.* this Day.

XVI.

QUHEN that he ſaw his blude ſae reid,
   To fle might nae Man let him,
He weind it had been for auld feid,
   He thocht ane cry'd, Haif at him.

                          He

He gart his Feit defend his Heid,
   The far fairer it fet him;
Quhyl he was paft out of all pleid,
   They fould bene fwift that gat him
Throw Speid, at, &c. that Day.

XVII.

THE Town-Soutar in Grief was bowdin,
   His Wyfe hang at his Waift;
His Body was in Blude all browdin,
   He graint lyk ony Ghaift.
Her Glitterand Hair that was fae gowden,
   Sae hard in Lufe him laift,
That for her Saik he was not zowden,
   Seven Myle that he was chaift,
And mair, &c. that Day.

XVIII.

THE Millar was of manly Mak,
   To meit him was nae Mows,
There durft not Ten cum him to tak,
   Sae noytit he thair Pows.

                              The

The Buſchment hale about him brak,
  And bikkert him with Bows,
Syne traytorly behind his Bak,
  They hewt him on the Hows,
Behind, at, *&c.* that Day.

XIX.

Twa that war Herdmen of the Herd,
  On udder ran lyk Rams,
Then followit Feymen, richt unaffeird,
  Bet on with Barrow trams,
But quhair thair Gobs thay war ungeird,
  They gat upon the Gams;
Quhyl bludy berkit war thair Baird,
  As they had worriet Lamms,
Maiſt lyk, at, *&c.* that Day.

XX. The

Hewt him on the Hows, Hew'd or cut him down, by ſtriking him behind on the *Houghs* or Hams.

Cum, Sum, &c., Come, Some. The *u* in Place of *o.*

Lamms, Thowme, Dum, &c., Lambs, Thumb, Dumb. The *b* ſeldom made Uſe of in ſuch Words.

XX.

THE Wyves keiſt up a hideous Zell,
    Quhen all thir Zounkers zokkit,
Als ferſs as ony Fyre-flauchts fell;
    Freiks to the Feilds they flokit.
The Carlis with Clubs did uder quell,
    Quhyl Blude at Breiſts out bokit;
Sae rudely rang the common Bell,
    That all the Steipill rokkit
For reid, at *Chryſts-Kirk* on the Grene that Day.

XXI.

QUHEN thay had beirt lyk baitit Bulls,
    And branewod brynt in Bails,
They wer as meik as ony Mulis,
    That mangit ar with Mails.

                                        For

Mulis, Mules. In ſeveral Words like this, where an *i* goes between an *l* and another Conſonant, we are to pronounce ſhort, as *Mules,* not *Mulis.*

Mangit ar with Mails, Maim'd with Burdens.

Flawchtir Fails, Turf that Country People flea for covering Houſes.

Haild the Dulis, is a Phraſe us'd at Foot Ball, or ſuch Games, where the Party that gains the *Dule* or Goal is ſaid to *hail* it, or win the Game.

For Faintneſs thae forfochtin Fulis,
  Fell down lyk flauchtir Fails:
Freſh Men came in and hail'd the Dulis,
  And dang them down in Dails,
Bedene, at, *&c.* that Day.

XXII.

Quhen all was done, *Dik* with an Aix,
  Came furth to fell a Fudder,
Quod he, quhair are zon hangit Smaiks,
  Richt now wald ſlain my Brudder.
His Wyfe bade him gae hame, *Gib Glaiks,*
  And ſae did *Meg* his Mudder.
He turn'd and gaif them baith their Paiks;
  For he durſt ding nane udder,
For Feir, at *Chryſt-Kirk* of the Grene that Day.

Finis quod King *JAMES* I.

                                    The

Fudder, properly a Load, relating to Lead. It is 1600 Pound
Weight: in our old Authors it often metaphorically means a great many.

✺✺✺✺✺✺✺✺✺✺

The THISTLE *and the* ROSE,
O'er Flowers and Herbage green,
By Lady Nature choſe,
Brave King and lovely Queen.

A

POEM

In Honour of

MARGARET, Daughter to *HENRY* the VII. of *England*, Queen to JAMES the IV. King of *SCOTS*.

I.

QUHEN *Merch* with variand Winds was overpaſt,
 And ſweit *Apryle* had with his Silver Showers
Tane Leif of Nature, with an orient Blaſt,
 And luſty *May*, that Mudder is of Flowrs,
 Had maid the Birds begin be tymous Hours;
Amang the tendir Odours reid and quhyt,
 Quhois Harmony to heir was grit Delyt.

II. IN

Luſty May, Deſireable *May.* Luſty, through theſe Poems, is an Epithet frequently us'd in this Senſe; alſo in our Language it expreſſes Youthful, Blooming, Large, Jolly.

II.

In Bed at Morrow, ſleiping as I lay,
   Methocht *Aurora* with her Rubie Ene,
In at my Window lukit by the Day,
   And halſit me, with Viſage pale and grene,
   Upon her Hand a Lark ſang frae the Splene,
Luvers, awake out of your Slumbering,
Se how the luſty Morning dois upſpring.

III.

Methocht freſh *May* before my Bed upſtood,
   In Weid depainted of ilk diverſe Hew,
Sober, benyng, and full of Menſuetude,
   In Bright Atyre of Flours, all forget new,
   Of heavenly Colour quhyt, reid, brown and blew,
Balmit in Dew, and gilt with Phebus Beims,
Quhyle all the Houſe ilumynt with her Leims.

IV.

Slugart, ſcho ſaid, awake annon, for Schame,
   And in my Honour ſumthing thou gae wryte;
The Lark has done, the merry Day proclaim,
   Luvers to rais with Comfort and Delyte,
   Will nocht increaſe thy Courage to indyt;
                       Quhaſe

Lukit by the Day, Looked in at my Window by Day or the Dawn-
ing. *Halſit,* Hail'd or Saluted.
Menſuetude, Mildneſs, or good Humour.

Quhaſe Heart ſomtyme has glad and bliſsful bene,
Sangs oft to mak under the Brenches grene.

V.

QUHERTO, quoth I, fall I upryſe at Morrow,
　For in thy Month few Birds haif I hard ſing,
Thay haif mair Cauſe to weip and plein their Sorrow:
　Thy Air it is not holſum nor benyng,
　Lord *Eolus* dois in thy Seaſon ring,
Sae bouſteous ar the blaſts of his ſhill horn,
Amang thy Bews to walk I haif forborn.

VI.

WITH that the Lady ſoberly did ſmyle,
　And ſaid, Upryſe and do thy Obſervance:
Thou did promiſt in *Mayis* luſty quhyle,
　Then to diſcryve the *ROSE* of moſt Pleſance.
　Go ſee the Birdis how they ſing and dance,
And how the Skyes iluminat ar bricht,
Enamylt richly with new azure Licht.

VII. QUHEN

Do thy Obſervance, Perform thy Duty or Reſpects. Here 'tis proper
we take notice of the Cadency of ſuch Words; many in that Age being
pronounced long that now are expreſſed ſhort: But our Union with
France, and *French* Auxiliaries ſo often in *Scotland* at that Time, can
eaſily account for that Manner of Pronunciation.

C

VII.

QUHEN this was ſaid, away then went the Quene,
   And entert in a luſty Garden gent;
And then methocht, full haſtylie beſene,
   In Sark and Mantle after her I went
   Into this Garth moſt dulce and redolent,
Of Herb and Flowir, and tender Plants moſt ſweit,
And grene Leivs doing of Dew doun fleit.

VIII.

THE pourpour Sun, with tender Rayis reid,
   In orient bricht as Angel did appeir,
Throu golden Skys advancing up his Heid,
   Whoſe gildet Treſſes ſchone ſae wonder cleir,
   That all the Warld tuke Comfort far and neir,
To luke upon his freſh and bliſsful Face,
Doing all ſable frae the Heavenis chace.

IX.

AND as the bliſsful Sun drave up the Sky,
   All Nature ſang throu Comfort of the Licht;
The Minſtrells wingd with open Voyces cry,
   O Luvers now is fled the dully Nicht,
   Come welcome Day that comforts every Wicht.

Hail

Hail *May*, hail *Flora*, hail *Aurora* ſhene,
Hail Princeſs Nature, hail Luves hartſome Quene.

X.

DAME Nature gave an Inhibition ther
   To *Neptune* ferſs and *Eolus* the bauld,
Not to perturb the Water nor the Air,
    That nowther blaſhy Shower, nor Blasts mair
      cauld
    Suld Flowirs effray nor Fowles upon the Fauld.
Scho bad eik *Juno* Goddes of the Sky,
That ſcho the Heaven ſuld keep amene and dry.

XI.

ALS ſcho ordaind that every Bird and Beiſt
   Before her Hieneſs ſuld annone compeir,
And every Flowir of Virtue maiſt and leiſt,
    And every Herb in fair Feild far and neir,
    As they had wont in *May* frae Yeir to Yeir:
To hir thair Quene to mak Obediens,
Full law inclynand with dew Reverens.

XII. WITH

Obediens and *Reverens*, as obſerved before in the Words *Obſervance*
and *Pleſance*, muſt be accented long.

XII.

WITH that annone ſcho ſent the ſwift fute *Roe*,
  To bring in alkind Beiſt frae Dale and Doun,
The reſtleſs *Swallow* ordert ſcho to go,
  And fetch all Fowl of ſmall and grit Renown,
  And to gar Flowirs appeir of all Faſſoun:
Fully craftely conjurit ſhe the *Yarrow*.
Quhilk did forth ſwirk as ſwift as ony Arrow.

XIII.

ALL brocht in were, in twynkling of an Ee,
  Baith *Beiſt* and *Bird* and *Flowir* before the *Quene*,
And firſt the *Lyon* greateſt of Degre
  Was ſummond ther, and he, fair to be ſene,
  With a full hardy Countenance and kene,
Before *Dam Nature* came, and did inclyne,
With Viſage bauld, and Courage Leonyne.

XIV. THIS

Courage Leonyne. This perhaps may be ſmil'd at, but there's as much Reaſon to laugh at the modern Phraſe of one's looking like himſelf.

XIV.

THIS awful Beift was terrible of Cheir,
    Perfing of Luke, and ftout of Countenance,
Right ftrong of Corps, of Faffon fair, bot feir,
    Lufty of Shape, licht of Deliverance,
    Reid of his Colour, as the Ruby Glance:
In Feild of Gold he ftude full rampantly,
With Flowr-de-Lyces circlet plefantly.

XV.

THIS *Lady* liftit up his Cluves fae cleir,
    And lute him liftlie lein upon hir Knee,
And crownit him with Diadem full deir,
    Of radyous Stanes maift ryall there to fee,
    Saying, The King of all Beifts mak I thee,
                     And

If one were to comment and illuftrate every poetical Beauty that
ftrikes our Imaginations fo agreeably, and come fo frequent, he would
fwell the Notes too much, and rob the Reader of a Pleafure which is
his own Property; wherefore fuch Annotations fhall be declined.
When Folks are ravifhed with any Pleafure tho' it be obvious to every
By-ftander, yet they cannot help expreffing what delights them many
Times over, when there is not the leaft Occafion for Information.
This was juft my Cafe, on reading this excellent Defcription of the Lyon
and the *Scots* Arms, never fo happily blazoned.

And the Protector cheif in Wodes and Schaws,
Go furth, and to thy Leiges keip the Laws.

XVI.

JUSTICE exerce, with Mercy and Conſciens,
    And let nae ſmall Beiſt ſuffir Skaith nor Skorns,
Of greiter Beiſts that bein of more Puſiance.
    Do Law alyke to Apes and Unicorns,
    And lat na Bowgle with his bouſteous Horns
Oppreſs the meik Pluch-Ox, for all his Pryd,
But in the Yok go quietly him beſyd.

XVII.

WHEN this was ſaid, with Noyſe and Sound of
    Joy,
    All Kynd of Quadrupeds in thair Degree,
Attains cry'd, *Laud,* and then, *Vive le Roy;*
    Syne at his Feit fell with Humility;
    To him they all made Homage and Feiltie;
And he did tham reſaif with princely Laits,
Whoſe noble Yre his Greitneſs mitigates.

XVIII.

SYNE crownit ſcho the *Eagle* King of Fowls;
    And ſharp as Darts of Steil ſcho made his Penns,
And bade him be as juſt to *Whawps* and *Owls,*

As

As unto *Peakoks, Papingos,* or *Crans,*
And mak ane Law for *wicht Fowls* and for *Wrens,*
And let nae Fowl of Rapine do affray,
Nor Birds devore but his own proper Prey.

XIX.

THEN callt fcho all the Flowirs grew in the Feild,
   Difcryving all thair Faffons and Effeirs,
Upon the awfull THISTLE fhe beheld,
   And faw him guarded with a Bufh of Speirs,
   Confiddering him fae able for the Weirs,
A radiant Crown of Rubies fcho him gaif,
And faid, in Feild go forth, and fend the laif.

XX.

AND fen thou art a King, be thou defcreit,
   Herb without Value hald not of fic Pryce,
As Herb of Vertew and of Odour fweet,
   And let no Netle vyle and full of Vyce
   Hir fallow with the gudly *Flowr-de-Lyce,*
Nor let no wyld Weid, full of Churlifhnefs,
Compare hir to the Lillys Nobilnefs.

XXI. NOR

XXI.

Nor hald nane other Flowir in ſic denty
　　As the freſh Rose, of Colour reid and quhyt;
For if thou dois, hurt is thyne Honeſty,
　　Conſiddering that no Flowir is ſae perfyte,
　　Sae full of Pleſans, Vertew and Delyte,
Sae full of bliſsful Angellyke Bewtie,
Imperial Birth, Honour and Dignitie.

XXII.

Then to the Rose ſcho did her Viſage turn,
　　And ſaid, O luſty Dochter moſt benyng,
Abofe the Lilly thou art iluſterous born,
　　Frae Ryal Linage ryſing freſh and yung,
　　But ony Spot or Macull doing ſprung:
Cum Blume of Joy with richeſt Jems be crownd,
For owre the laif thy Bewtie is renound.

XXIII.

A coſtly Crown with Stanes clarified bricht,
　　This comely Quene did on hir Heid incloſe,
Quhyle all the Land illumynat of Licht;
　　　　　　　　　　　　　　　　　Quhairfor

Quhois, Dois, Hir, &c., Whoſe, Does, Her. The *e* in many ſuch
Words is ſupplied with *i.*
But ony Spot, Without Spot.

Quhairfor methocht, the Flowirs did all rejoſe,
Crying attaines, Hail to the fragrant Rose,
Hail Empreſs of the Herbs, freſch Quene of Flowirs,
To the be Glore and Honour at all Hours.

XXIV.

Then all the Birds thay ſang with Voice on hicht,
    Whoſe mirthfull Sound was marvellous to heir;
The Mavys ſang, Hail Rose moſt rich and richt,
    That does upfluriſs under *Phebus* Sphere,
    Hail Plant of Youth, Hail Princes Dochter deir,
Hail Bloſome breking out of Blude Ryal,
    Quhois precious Vertew is Imperial.

XXV.

The Merle ſcho ſang, Hail Rose of moſt Delyt,
    Hail of all Flowirs the ſweit and ſoverain Quene:
The Lark ſcho ſang, Hail Rose baith reid and quhyt,
    Moſt pleſand Flowir of michty Colours twain;
    Nichtingails ſang, Hail Nature's Suffragane,
In Bewty, Nurture, and each Nobilneſs,
In rich Array, Renown and Gentilneſs.

XXVI. The

That the Houſe of *York* and *Lancaſter* (the *White* and *Red Roſe*) were
united in the Perſon of our Queen, is well known.

XXVI.

THE common Voice upraiſe of Birdis ſmall,
  Upon this Ways, O bliſſit be the Hour
That thou was choſe to be our Principal,
    Welcome to be our Princes crownd with Powir,
    Our Perle, our Pleſance, and our Paramour,
Our Peace, our Play, our plain Felicity:
CHRYST the conſerve from all Adverſity.

XXVII.

THEN all the Conſort ſang with ſic a Shout,
  That I anone awakent quhair I lay,
And with a Braid I turnit me about
    To ſe this Court, but all wer gone away;
    Then up I leint me, halflings in affray,
Callt to my Muſe, and for my Subjeck choſe
To ſing the Ryal THISTLE and the ROSE.

Quod Mr. Wᵐ· DUNBAR.

A

A
PANYGYRICK
ON
Sr Penny.

I.

Richt fain wald I my Qwaintance mak
    Sr *Penny* with, and wate ye quhy?
He is a Man will undertak
    A Lairdſhip of braid Lands to buy;
    Thairfoir methink richt fain wald I
With him in Fellowſhip repair,
    Becauſe he is in Company
A noble Gyde baith late and air.

II. Sr

II.

Sʀ *Penny* for till hald in Hand,
   His Company they think fae fweit;
Sum does not care to fell thair Land,
   With gude Sr *Penny* for to meit,
   Becaufe he is of a noble Spreit,
A furthy Man and a forfeiand;
   There is no Mater ends compleit,
Till he fet to his Seil and Hand.

III.

Sʀ *Penny* is a valiant Man,
   Of mekle Strenth and Dignitie,
And evir fen this Warld began,
   In this Land autoreift is he:
   The King or Quene ze may not fee,
They ftill fo tenderlie him trete,
   That ther can nathing endit be,
Without his Company ze get.

IV.

Sʀ *Penny* is a Man of Law,
   And (witt ye weil) baith wyfe and war;
He mony Reafons can furth fchaw,
   Quhen he is ftanding at the Bar,

Is

Is nane fae fharp that can him fcar,
Quhen he propons furth ony Pley;
　Nor zit fae hardy Man as dar
Sr *Penny* tyne or difobey.

V.

Sᴿ *Penny* is baith leird and wyfe,
　The Kirk to fteir he taks in Hand,
Difponer of ilk Benefice
　In this Realm, throu all the Land;
　Is nane fae wicht dar him gainftand,
Sae wyfely can Sr *Penny* wirk;
　And als Sr *Symonie* his Servand,
That now is Gydar of the Kirk.

VI.

Gɪꜰ to the Court thou mak repair,
　And ther haif Matters to proclame,
Thou art unable weil to fair,
　Sr *Penny* gif thou leif at hame,
　To bring him furth think thou nae Schame;
I do thee weil to underftand,
　Into thy Bag beir thou his Name,
Thy Matter cums better to hand.

VII. Sᴿ

VII.

Sʀ *Penny* now is maid an Owll,
   They wirk him mekle Tray and Tene,
They hald him in till he hair-moull,
   And maks him blind of baith his Ene;
   Thirout he is but ſindle ſene,
Sae faſt tharin they can him ſteik,
   That Commons pure cannot obtain
Ane Day to byd with him and ſpeik.

Tray and *Tene*, Anger.
Hair-moull, Grown hoary with Mouldineſs.

VERTUE

VERTUE and VYCE.

A

POEM;

Addreſt to

JAMES V. *King of* SCOTS,

By the famous and renown'd Clerk,

Mr. JOHN BELLENTYNE,

Arch-Dean of Murray.

———oo———

I.

QUHEN Silver *Diane* full of Beims bricht,
　　Frae dark Eclips was paſt this uther Nicht,
And to the Crab hir proper Manſion gane；
Artophilax contending with his Micht
In the grit Eiſt to ſet his Viſage richt；
　　I mene the Leider of the *Charle-wane:*
Aboif our Heid then was the *Urſis* twain,
Quhen Starris ſmall obſcure grew to our Sicht,
　　And *Lucifer* left twinkling him alane.

II. THE

II.

THE frofty Nicht with her prolixit Hours,
Her Mantle quhyt fpred on the tender Flours;
　　When ardent Labour has addreffit me,
Tranflate the Tale of our Progenitours,
Thair greit Manheid, Wifdom and hie Honours,
　　Quhair we may cleir, as in a Mirrour, fee
　　The furious End fomtymes of Tyranie;
Somtymes the Gloir of prudent Governours,
　　Ilk State appryfit in thair Facultie.

III.

MY weary Spreit defiring to reprefs
My emptive Pen of frutelefs Biffinefs,
　　Awalkit forth to tak the recent Air,
When *Priapus* with ftormy Weid opprefs,
Requeiftit me, in his maift Tendernefs,
　　To reft a while amids his Gardens bare.
　　But I no maner coud my Mynd prepare
To fet afyde unplefant Havynefs
　　On this and that contempling Solitare.

IV. AND

Priapus, who prefides over Gardens.

IV.

AND firſt occurrt to my remembering,
How that I was in Service with the King,
   Put to his Grace in Zeirs tendereſt,
Clerk of his Compts, althocht I was inding,
With Heart and Hand, and evry uther thing,
   That micht him pleiſe in ony manner beſt,
   While Envy grit me from his Service keſt,
By them that had the Court in governing,
   As Bird bot Plumes is herryt of her Neſt.

V.

OUR Lyfe, our Gyding, and our Aventuris,
Dependance have on thir celeſt Creaturis,
   Apperandly by ſome Neceſſitie;
For thocht a Man wald ſet his biſſy curis,
Sae far as Labour and his Wiſdom furis,
   To flie hard Chance of Infortunitie,
   Tho he eſchew it with Difficultie,
The curſid Weird yet ithandly enduris,
   Gien to him firſt in his Nativitie.

VI. OF

D

VI.

OF eardlie State bewailing thus the Chance
Of Fortune gude I had nae Efperance,
 Sae lang I had fwomt in hir Seis fae deip,
That fad Avyfing with her thochtfull Lance
Coud find nae Port to anker her Firmance,
 Till *Morpheus* the dreiry God of Sleip,
 For very Rewth did on my Cures weip,
And fet his Slewth and deidly Countenance,
 With fnorand Vains to throw my Body creip.

VII.

METHOCHT I was into a plefand Meid,
Quhair *Flora* made the tender Bluims to fpreid
 Throw kindly Dew, and Humours nutrative,
Quhen golden *Titan* with his Flamis fae reid,
Aboif the Seis upraift his glorious Heid,
 Defounding down his Heit reftorative
 To evry Fruit that Nature maid to live,
Whilk was afore into the Winter deid,
 With Stormis cauld, and Har-froft penetrive.

VIII. A

VIII.

A Silver Fountain fprang with Watir cleir
Into that Place, quhair I approchit neir;
 Quhair I did fone efpy a fellon Reird
Of courtly Gallants in thair gayeft Weir,
Rejoycing them in Seafon of the Zeir,
 As it had bene of *Mayis* fweit Day the Feird,
 Their gudelie Havings made me nocht affeird;
With them I faw a crownit King appeir,
 With tender Downs arrifing on his Beird.

IX.

THIR courtly Gallants fettand thair Intents
To fing and play on divers Inftruments;
 According to this PRINCIS Appetyte,
Twa Ladyis fair came pranfand owre the Bents,
Thair coftly Cleathing fhawd their mighty Rents;
 Quhat Heart micht wifh, they wanted not a Myte,
 The Rubies fhone upon thair Fingers quhyt:
And finaly I knew by thair Confents
 This VERTUE was, that uther hecht *Delyte.*

X. THIR

X.

Thir Goddeſſes arrayt in this fine Ways,
As Reverence and Honour liſt devyſe,
   Afore this Prince fell down upon thair Kneis,
Syne dreſt themſells into thair beſt Avyſe,
Sae far as Wiſdom in thair Powir lyes,
   To do the Thing that micht him beſt appleiſe,
   Quhair he rejoyced in his heavenly Gleis,
And him deſyret that for his Emperyſs,
   Ane of them twa unto his Lady cheis.

XI.

And firſt *Delyte* unto the Prince ſaid thus,
Maiſt valiant Knycht, in Actions amorous,
   And luſtyeſt that evir Nature wrocht,
Quha in the Flour of Zouth mellyfluous,
With Notes ſweit, and ſang mellodious,
   Awalketh heir amang the Flowirs ſoft,
   Thou has nae Game, but in thy mirry Thocht,
My heavenly Bliſs is ſo delicious,
   All Wealth in Eard bot it availeth nocht.

XII. Tho

XII.

Tho thou had *France*, and all beyont the *Po*,
Spain, *Ingland*, *Pole*, with uther Kingdoms moe,
   And reign oure them in State moſt glorious,
Thy puſſiant Empyre is not worth a Stro,
Gif it unto thy Pleiſurs is a Foe,
    Or pains thy Mind with Cares are dolourus;
    Ther is nathing may be ſae odious
To Man, as leif in Miſery and Woe,
   Defrauding God of Nature *Genius.*

XIII.

Dress thee thairfor with all thy biſſy Cure,
That thou in Joy and Pleiſure may endure;
   Be Sicht of thir four Bodyis elementar,
Twa groſs and heavy, twa are licht and pure,
Thir Elements be working of Nature,
    In uther change; and tho they be richt far
    Frae uther twind, with Qualitys contrair,
Of them are made all Creatures Eard eir bure,
   And finaly in them reſolvit ar.

XIV. The

XIV.

THE Fyre in Air, the Air in Watter cleir,
In Eard the Watter turns withouten Weir,
   The Eard in Watter it turns ower again;
Sae furth in Order nochts confumed heir,
And Man new born begins sone to appeir
   Ane uther Figure than afore was tane,
   Quhen he is deid, the Matter does remain,
Tho it refolve into fum new Manner,
   Naething is new, nocht but the Form is gane.

XV.

THUS naething is in Eard but fugitive,
Paffand and command fpreiding fucceffive;
   And as a Beift, fo is a Man confave
Of Seid infufd in Members genitive,
And furth his Tyme in Plefoure does out dryve
   As Chance him leids, till he be laid in Grave:
   Thairfor thy Hevin and Plefour now refave,
Quhile thou art heir into this prefent Lyve,
   For after Death thou fall no Plefour haif.

XVI. THE

XVI.

The Rose, the Lilly, and the Violet,
Unpult, fone wither, and with winds owrefet,
   Wallout falls down bot ony Fruit, I wifs,
Thairfore I fay, Sen that naething may let,
But thy bricht Hew maun be with Zeirs all fret,
   (For every Thing but for a Seafon is)
   Thou may not haif a mair excellent Blifs
Than ly all Nicht into my Arms plet,
   To hals and brais with mony a lufty Kifs.

XVII.

And haif my tender Body by thy Syde,
So proper fet, quhilk Nature has provyde
   With every Plefour, that thou mayft divyne,
Ay quhile my tender Zeirs be overflyde;
Then gif thou pleis that I thy Brydel gyde,
   Thou maun allways from agit men declyne,
   Syne drefs thy Hairt, thy Courage and Ingyne,
To fuffer nane fall in thy Houfe abyde,
   But gif thay will unto thy Luft inclyne.

XVIII. Gif

XVIII.

GIF thou defyres into the Seis to fleit
Of hevinly Blifs, than me thy Lady treit;
　For it is faid by Clerks of fair Renown,
Thair is nae Pleafour in this Eard fo grit,
As quhen a Luver dois his Lady meit,
　To raife his Lyf frae mony a deidlie Soun,
　As hieft plefour but Comparifoun.
I fall the geif in thy Zeirs zoung and fweit,
　A lufty Halk with mony Plumes full broun.

XIX.

QUHILK fall be found fae joyous and Plefant,
Gif thou into her mirry Flichts fall hant,
　Of evry Blifs that may in Eard appeir,
As Hairt will think thou fall nae Plenty want,
Quhile Zeirs fwift with Quheils properant,
　Confume thy Strenth, and all thy Bewtie cleir.
　And quhen *Delyt* had faid on this Maner,
As Rage of Zowtheid thocht maift relivant;
　Then *Vertew* fpake, as after ye fall heir.

XX. MY

XX.

My Lands full braid with mony a plenteous Shyre,
Sall give thy Hienefs, (gif thou lift difyre)
 Triumphant Glore, hie Honour, Fame divyne,
With fic Puiffance, that them nae furious Yre,
Nor weirand Age, nor Flames of birnand Fyre,
 Nor bitter Death may bring unto Rewyne,
 But thou maun firft enfuffer meikle Pyne,
Abune thy felf, that thou may haif Empyre,
 Then fall thy Fame and Honour haif no Fyne.

XXI.

Amang my Faes my Realms fet ar all,
Quhilk haif with me a Weir continual,⁻
 And ever ftill dois on my Border ly :
And tho' thay may nae Ways me overthrawl,
Thay ly in wait, gif ony Chance may fall,
 Of me fumtyme to get the Victory.
 Thus is my Lyfe an ithand Chevalry,
And Labour halds me ftrong as ony Wall,
 And nathing breks me but vyl Slugardy.

XXII. Nae

XXII.

Nae Fortune may againſt me ocht avail,
Tho ſcho with cloudy ſtorms me aft aſſail.
   I brek the Streim of ſharp adverſity,
In Wedder lown, and maiſt tempeſtous Hail,
Bot any Dreid I beir an equal Sail:
    My Ships ſae ſtrong, that I may never die,
    Wit, Reaſon, Manheid governs me ſae hie,
Nae influence of Starns can eir prevail
   To rigne owre me with Infortunitie.

XXIII.

The Rage of Zouth can never dantit be,
Bot grit Diſtreſs and ſharp Adverſity,
   As be this Reaſon is experience;
The fyneſt Gold or Silver that we ſe,
May not be wrocht to our Utility,
    Without kein Flames and bitter Violence;
    The mair Diſtreſs, the mair Intelligence.
Quha eir fails lang in hie Proſperity,
   Ar ſune owreſet, gainſt ſtorms have nae Defence.

XXIV. This

XXIV.

This fragill Lyfe, as Moment induring,
Bot doubt fall thee and all the Warld bring
   To ficker Blifs, or then eternal Wae.
Gif thou by honeft Labour dois a Thing,
Thy Labour vaniefis but tarrying;
   Howbeit thy honeft Warks they do not fae.
   Gif thou does ocht of Luft be Nicht or Day,
The fhameful Deid, without differering,
   Continues ftill when Plefour is away.

XXV.

As Carvell ticht, faft tending throw the Sie,
Leives nae imprent amang the Wallis hie.
   As fwifteft Birds with mony a biffy Plume
Perfis the Air, and wates not quhair thay flie,
Sicklyks our Lyfe without Activitie;
   It giffes na Fruit, howbeit a Shadow blume.
   Quha dois thair Lyfe in Ydlenefs confume,
Bot Vertews Deids, thair Fame and Memorie
   Sall vanife foner than the reiky Fume.

XXVI. As

XXVI.

As Watter purges and maks Bodys fair,
As Fyre afcends be Nature in the Air,
 And purefies with Heit thats vehement:
As Flowir does fmell, as Fruit is nurifare:
As precious Balmes reverts the Things ar fair,
 And maks them of the Rot impatient.
 As Spyce maift fweit, and Rofe maift redolent;
As ftern of Day by Motion circulair,
 Chaifes the Nicht with Beims refplendent.

XXVII.

SICKLYKE my Warks they perfyt every Wicht,
In fervent Luve of maift excellent Licht,
 And maks a Man into this Eard bot Peir,
And does the Saul frae all Disorder dicht,
With Odour dulce, and maks it ftill mair bricht
 Than *Diane* full, or zet *Apollo* cleir,
 Syn raifes it into the hieft Sphere,
Immortally to fhine in GODS awin Sicht,
 His chofen Creature, and as Spous maift deir.

XXVIII. THIS

XXVIII.

THIS uther Wretch that clipit is *Delyte*,
Involves Mankynd be fenfual Appityte,
  In every Kind of Vyce and Miferie,
Because nae Wit nor Reafon is perfyte
Quhair fhe is Gyde, but Skaith thats infinyt;
    With Dolour, Shame, and urgent Povertie;
    For fcho fprang frae the licht Froth of the Se.
Quhilk fignifies hir Plefour venomit,
    Is minglit ay with fhairp Adverfitie.

XXIX.

DUKE *Hannibal*, as mony Authors wrait,
Throw *Spenzie* came be mony a Paffage ftrait;
  To *Italy* in Furor bellical,
Brak down hie Walls, and hieft Mountains flait,
And to his Army made an open Gait,
    And Victories had on the *Romans* all.
    At *Capua* by Plefour fenfual,
The Duke was made fae faft and delicate,
    That by his Faes he was fone overthrawll.

XXX. OF

XXX.

OF ferſs *Achill* the weirly Deids ſprang,
In *Troy* and *Greice*, quhylè he in VERTUE rang,
  How Luſt him ſlew it is but Rewth to heir:
Siclyk the *Trojans* with thair Knichts ſtrang,
The valiant *Greiks* furth frae thair Ruins dang,
  Victoriouſly exercit mony a Zeir;
  That Nicht they went to thair Luſt and Pleſour,
The fatal Horſs did throw thair Walls fang,
  Quhais pregnant Sydes wer full of Men of Weir.

XXXI.

SARDANAPALL, that Prince efeminat,
Frae Deids of Knichts baſely degenerat,
  Twynand the Threid of whyt or purpour Lint,
With Fingers ſaft amang the Ladyis ſat,
And with his Luſt couth not be ſatiate,
  Till frae his Faes came laſt the bitter Dint.
  Quhat nobil Men and Ladyis haif bene tint,
Quhen they with Luſt have bene intoxicat,
  To ſchaw at lenth my Tung wald nevir ſtint.

XXXII. BUT

XXXII.

But brave *Camil* the valiant Chevalier,
(When he the *Gauls* had dantint be his Weir)
   Of Heritage wald haif nae Recompence;
For gif his Bairns, his Kin and Friends maiſt deir
Were verteous, they could not fail ilk Zeir
   To haif enough, be *Roman* Providence.
   Gif they wer given to Vyce and Inſolence,
It was not neidfull he ſould conqueiſs Geir,
   To be the Cauſe of thair Incontinence.

XXXIII.

Sum nobil Men, as Poets liſt declair,
Were Deifeit, ſum made Gods of the Air,
   Sum of the Heaven, as *Eolus, Vulcan,*
Apollo, Saturn, Hermes, Jupiter,
Mars, Hercules, and uther Men preclair,
   That Fame imortall in this Warld wan:
   Quhy wer thir People called Gods than?
Becauſe they had a Vertue ſingulair,
   Excellent hie abune the Ingyne of Man.

XXXIV. And

XXXIV.

AND uthers are in Reik fulphurious,
As *Ixion*, and weiry *Syfyphus*,
   Eumenides, the Furys odibil,
The proud Gyants, and thrifty *Tantalus*,
With ugly Drink, and Fude maift vennomus,
   Quhair Flames bauld, and Mirknefs ar fenfibil:
   Quhy ar thir Folk in Pains fae terribil?
Becaufe they were but Shrews maift vicious
   Into thair Lyfe, with Deids maift horribil.

XXXV.

AND tho nae Fruit wer after confequent
Of mortall Lyfe, but for this Warld prefent
   Ilk Man to haif allenerlie Refpect;
Zet VERTUE fould frae Vice be different,
As quick frae deid, as rich frae indigent;
   That ane to hieft Honour does direct,
   This uther Saul and Body does neglect.
That ane of Reafon maift intelligent,
   This uther of Beifts following the Effect.

XXXVI. FOR

XXXVI.

For he that nold againft his vyl Lufts ftryve,
But lives as Beifts of Knawlege fenfityve,
  Grows faft to Eild, and Death him fone owrehails:
Thairfor the Mule is of a langer Lyfe
Than the ftaind Horfe; alfo the barrand Wyfe
  Zouthfull appeirs, when that the Brudie fails:
  We alfo fe when Nature nocht prevails,
The Pain and Dolour ar fae pungityve,
  Nae Medycyne the Patient then avails.

XXXVII.

Sen our Intents baith we haif fhawn thee thus,
Cheis of us twae the maift delicious,
  Or to fuftene a fharp Adverfitie,
Danting the Rage of Zouth-heid furious,
And fyn poffes Triumphs innumerous,
  With hie Empyre, and lang Felicitie;
  Or haif ane Moment Senfualitie
Of fulifh Zouth, in Lyf voluptous,
  And all thy Days full of fad Miferie.

XXXVIII. *PHE-*

E

XXXVIII.

PHEBUS be this his fyrie Cart did wry,
Frae South to Weſt declynand biſſyly
   To dip his Steids into the Weſtlin Main;
When ryſing Damps owreſaild his Viſage dry
With Vapours thick, and cluddet all the Sky,
    And *Notus* brym, the Wind meridian,
    With Wings donk, and Fedders full of Rain,
Awakent me, that I could not eſpy
   Quhilk of the twa was for his Lady tane.

XXXIX.

But ſone I knew they were the Goddeſſes
That came in Sleip to valiant *Hercules,*
   When he was zung, and free of every Lore,
To Luſt or Honour, Purtith or Riches,
Quhair he contempnit Luſt and Idleneſs,
    That he in Vertue micht his Lyfe decore;
    Then Warks he did of maiſt excellent Glore;
The mair increſt his painfull Biſſineſs,
   His hie Triumphs and Loving was the more.

A

A Bytand BALLAT on warlo Wives,
That gar thair Men live pinging Lives.

I.

BE merry, Brethrene, ane and all,
    And fet all Sturt afide;
And every ane togither call
    To God to be our Gyd;
For as lang lives the mirry Man,
As dois the Wretch for ocht he can,
When Deid him ftrakes, he wats na whan,
    And charges him to byde.

II.

THE Rich then fall not fpared be,
    Thocht they haif Gold and Land,
Nor zit the Fair, for their Bewty,
    Cannot that Charge gainftand.

Tho

Tho Wicht or Weak wald flee away,
Nae Doubt but all maun Ranfom pay,
Quhat Place or quhare can nae Man say,
  Be Se or zit be Land.

III.

THE mirryeft Man that leives on Lyfe,
 He fails upon the Se;
For he knaws neither Sturt nor Stryfe,
 But blyth and glad is he:
But he that has an evil Wyfe,
Has Sour and Sorrow all his Lyfe,
And that Man quilk leives ay in Stryf,
  How can he mirry be?

IV.

ANE evil Wyfe is the warft aught
 That ony Man can haif;
For he may nevir fit in Saught,
 Unlefs he be her Slaif:

        But

But of that Sort I knaw nane uther,
Except a Cuckald or his Bruther;
Sunt Lairds and Cuckalds altogither, .
     May wifs their Wyves in Graif.

V.

BECAUSE thair Wyves haif Maiftery,
    That they dar naeways cheip,
But gif it be in Privity,
    Quhen they are faft afleip;
Ane mirry in thair Company,
To them is worth baith Gold and Fie:
A Menftrell neir coud dairthful be,
     Thair Mirth if he coud beit.

VI.

BUT of that Sort whilk I report,
    I knaw nane in this Ring:
But we may all baith grit and fmall,
    Glaidly baith dance and fing,

                    Quha

Sunt Lairds. Here is spelled with an *S*, as it ought, and not with a *C*, as many of the *Englifh* do.

Quha lifts not here to make gude Cheir,
Perchance his Guids an uthir Yeir
Be fpent, quhen he is brought to Beir,
   Quhen his Wyfe taks the Fling.

VII.

It has been fene, that wyfe Women,
 After their Hufband's Deid,
Has gotten Men has gart them ken,
 If they could bear a Laid.
With a grene Sting, hes gart them bring
The Geir that won was by a Dring;
And fyne gart all the Bairnies fing,
   Ramukloch in their Bed.

VIII.

Then wad fcho fay, Alake this Day,
 For him that wan this Geir,
Quhen I him had, I fkairfly faid,
 My Heart anes mak gude Cheir.
Or I had letten him fpend a Plak,
I lure haif witten him brake his Bak,
Or els his Craig had gotten a Crak,
   Ower the Hicht of the Stair.

        IX. Ze

IX.

Ze Niggarts then Example tak,
    And leir to ſpend your awn,
And with gude Freynds ay mirry mak,
    That it may well be knawn,
That thou art he quha wan this Geir;
And for thy Wyfe ſe thou nocht ſpair,
With blyth Freynds ay to make Repair,
    Sae ſall thy Worth be ſhawn.

X.

FINIS quod I, quha sets not by
    The ill Wyves of this Toun,
Tho for Diſpyte with me wald flyte,
    Gif thay micht put me doun.
Gif they wald ken quha maid this Sang,
Quhidder they will him heid or hang,
Flemyings his Name quhair eir he gang,
    In Country and in Toun.
                    Quod FLEMYNG.

Sets not by, Does not Value.   *Put doun*, Murder.

ROBIN

ROBIN *and* MAKYNE,

A PASTORAL.

I.

ROBIN ſat on the gude grene Hill,
    Keipand a Flock of Fie,
Quhen mirry *Makyne* ſaid him till,
    O *Robin* rew on me.
I haif thee luivt baith loud and ſtill,
    Thir Towmonds twa or thre;
My Dule in dern but gif thou dill,
    Doubtleſs bot Dreid I die.

II.

ROBIN replied, Now by the Rude,
    Naithing of Luve I knaw,
But keip my Sheip undir yon Wod,
    Lo quhair they raik on Raw.

Quhat

Dule in dern, Sorrow in ſecret.   *Dill,* ſtill, calm, or mitigate.
Raik on Raw, go apace in a Row.

Quhat can have mart thee in thy Mude,
　Thou *Makyne* to me fchaw?
Or quhat is Luve, or to be lude?
　Fain wald I leir that Law.

III.

THE Law of Luve gin thou wald leir,
　Tak thair an A, B, C;
Be keynd, courtas, and fair of Feir,
　Wyfe, hardy, kind and frie,
Sae that nae Danger do the deir,
　What dule in dern thou drie;
Prefs ay to pleis, and blyth appeir,
　Be patient, and privie.

IV.

ROBIN he anfwert her again,
　I wat not quhat is Luve,
But I haif Marvell uncertain
　Quhat maks thee thus wanrufe.

　　　　　　　　　　The

Fair of Feir, of a fair and healthful Look.

The Wedderis fair, and I am fain;
   My Sheip gaes hail abuve,
Gif we ſould play us on the Plain,
   They wald us baith repruve.

V.

ROBIN tak tent unto my Tale,
   And do all as I reid ;
And thou ſall haif my Heart all hale,
   Eik and my Maidenheid :
Sen GOD he ſends Bute for Bale,
   And for Murning Remeid.
I dern with thee, but give I dale,
   Doubtleſs I am but deid.

VI.

MAKYNE the Morn be this ilk Tyde,
   Gif ye will meit me heir,
May be my Sheip may gang besyde,
   Quhyle we have liggd full neir ;

                                       But

Wedderis, Weather's. It is to be noticed, that our Elders never apoſtrophiſed, yet by this one may judge that in every like Caſe they pronounced, as if ſuch Vowels were cut off with an Apoſtrophe: Without allowing this, many of their Lines will not be Numbers.

But maugre haif I, gif I byde,
    Frae thay begin to fteir,
Quhat lyes on Heart I will nocht hyd,
    Then *Makyn* mak gude Cheir.

VII.

ROBIN thou reivs me of my Reft;
    I luve but thee alane.
Makyne, adieu, the Sun goes Weft,
    The Day is neir-hand gane.
Robin in Dule I am fo dreft,
    That Luve will be my Bane.
Makyne gae luve quhair eir ye lift;
    For Lemans I luid nane.

VIII.

ROBIN I ftand in fic a Style,
    I fich, and that full fair.
Makyne I have been heir this quyle,
    At hame I wifh I were.
Robin, my Hinny, talk and fmyle,
    Gif thou will do nae mair.
Makyne sum uther Man beguyle;
    For hameward I will fare.

IX. SYNE

IX.

SYNE *Robin* on his Ways he went,
    As light as Leif on Tree:
But *Makyne* murnt and made Lament,
    Scho trow'd him neir to fee.
Robin he brayd attowre the Bent.
    Then *Makyne* cryd on hie,
Now may thou fing, for I am fhent!
    Quhat can ail Luve at me?

X.

MAKYNE went hame withouten fail,
    And weirylie could weip;
Then *Robin* in a full fair Dale
    Affemblit all his Sheip,
Be that fomepart of *Makyns* Ail,
    Outthrow his Heart coud creip,
Hir faft he followt to affail,
    And till her tuke gude keip.

                     XI. ABYD

Brayd attowre the Bent, hafted over the Field. *Tuke gude Keip,*
kept a clofe Eye upon her.

XI.

Abyd, abyd, thou fair *Makyne*,
  A Word for ony Thing;
For all my Luve it fall be thyne,
  Withoutten departing,
All hale thy Heart for till have myne,
  Is all my coveting;
My Sheip quhyle Morn till the Hours Nyne,
  Will mifter nae keiping.

XII.

ROBIN, thou has heard fung and fay,
  In Jefts and Storys auld,
The Man that will not when he may,
  Sall have nocht when he wald.
I pray to Heaven baith Nicht and Day,
  Be eikd their Cares fae cauld,
That preffes firft with thee to play,
  Be Forreft, Firth or Fauld.

XIII.

MAKYNE, the Nicht is foft and dry,
  The Wether warm and fair,
And the grene Wod richt neir hand by
  To walk attowre all where:

There

There may nae Janglers us efpy,
 That is to Luve contrair,
Therin, *Makyne*, baith you and I,
 Unſeen may mak Repair.

XIV.

ROBIN, that Warld is now away,
 And quyt brocht till an End,
And neir again thereto perfay,
 Sall it be as thou wend;
For of my Pain thou made but Play,
 I Words in vain did ſpend;
As thou has done ſae ſall I ſay,
 Murn on, I think to mend.

XV.

MAKYNE, the Hope of all my Heal,
 My Heart on thee is ſet;
I'll evermair to thee be leil,
 Quhile I may live but lett,
Never to fail as uthers feil,
 Quhat Grace ſo eir I get.
Robin, with thee I will not deal;
 Adieu, for this we met.

XVI. MA-

XVI.

MAKYNE went hameward blyth enough,
  Outowre the Holtis Hair.
Pure *Robin* murnd and *Makyne* leugh;
  Scho fang, and he fichd fair:
Scho left him in baith Wae and Wreuch,
  In Dolor and in Care,
Keipand his Herd under a Heuch,
  Amang the rafhy Gair.

Finis quod Mr. ROB. HENRYSON.

Advice

Advice to Man to enjoy his ain.

I.

MAN, fen thy Lyfe is ay in Weir,
  And Deid is ever drawing neir,
The Tyme unfiker and the Place,
Thyne ain Gude fpend quhile thou has Space.

II.

GIF it be thyne, thy felf it ufes,
Gif it be not, thee it refufes,
Another of thee Profit has,
Then fpend thy ain quhile thou has Space.

III.

THOU may to Day have Gude to fpend,
In haift to Morn may from it wend,
And leive an uther thy Baggs to brace,
Then fpend thy ain quhile thou has Space.

IV. QUHILE

IV.

QUHILE thou has Space, fe thou difpone
That for thy Geir: quhen thou art gone,
Nae Wicht ane other flay or chace,
Enjoyt thy felf quhile thou has Space.

V.

SUM all his Days dryves owre in vain,
Ay gatherand Geir with Greif and Pain,
Is nevir glade at *Zule* nor *Pais;*
Thyne ain Gude fpend quhile thou has Space.

VI.

SYNE cums ane blythfome of his Sorrow,
That for him prayd nor Even nor Morrow,
And fangs it all with Merrynefs;
Then fpend thy ain quhile thou has Space.

VII.

SUM gathers Gude, and ay it fpares,
And after him cum braw young Airs,
That his auld Thrift fets on an Ace,
And fendft a Sheiring in fhort Space.

VIII. ITS

F

VIII.

Its juſt all thyne that here thou ſpends,
And not all that on thee depends,
But his to ſpend it that has Grace;
Then ſpend thyn ain quhyle thou has Space.

IX.

Trust not annother will do ye to,
It that thy ſelf wald nevir do;
For gif thou dois, ſtrange is thy Cace;
Thine ain Gude ſpend quhyle thou has Space.

X.

Luke how the Bairn dois to the Mother,
And tak Example be nane uther,
That it not after be thy Caſe;
Sae ſpend thy ain quhyle thou has Space.

Quod Dumbar.

On

On a bonny Veſſel called THE FLEMING
BARK, *belonging to* Edinburgh.

I.

I HAVE a little FLEMING Berge
   Of cleanly Wark, and ſcho is wicht;
Quhat Pylot taks my Schip in Charge,
   Maun hald her cleanly, trim and ticht:
   Hir Hatches maun be handlit richt,
With Steir Burd, Baburd, Luf and Lie;
   Scho will ſail all the Winter Nicht,
And nevir tak a Tellzevie.

II.

WITH ane even Keil afore the Wind,
   Scho is richt fairdy with a Sail;
But at a Lufe ſcho lyis behind,
   Gar heis her quhile her Howbands ſkail;

Draw

Draw weil the tackle to her Tail,
Scho will not mifs to lay zour Maft,
To pump as aft as ze may fail,
Ze will neir hald her Watter-faft.

III.

To colf hir aft, can do no ill,
    And talloun quhair the Flude-mark flows;
But gif fcho lekks, get Men of Skill
    To ftap the Holes laigh in the Hows:
    For faut of Hemp, tak hairy Tows,
And Stane-balaft withouten other,
    In moonlefs Nichts it is nae Mows,
Except a ftout Man fteir the Ruther.

IV.

A Veffell fair abune the Watter,
    And is but laitly reikit too,
Quhairto till deave ze with hir Blatter
    Are nane fic in the Flot as fcho:
    Plum weil the Grund, quhat eir ze do, ·
Hail on the Fore-fheit and the Blind;
    Scho will tak in at Cap and Ko,
Without fcho balaft be behind.

                              V. NAE

V.

NAE Pedders Pak fcho will refufe,
  Altho hir Travel fcho fhoud tine,
Nae Cuckold Carle or Carlings Pet,
  That dois their Corn and Catle trayn;
  And quhere scho finds a Fallow fyne,
He will be fraught free for a Sowfe,
  She carries nocht but Men and Wyne,
And Bulion to the Cunzie-Houfe.

VI.

FOR Merchand Men I may haif Money,
  But nane fic as I wald defyre,
And I am laith to mell with ony,
  To leif my Matter in the Myre;
  That man that wirks beft for his Hyre
Its he fall be my Marriner,
  But Nicht and Day he maunna tyre
That fails my bonny Ballenger.

VII.

QUHEN Anker-hald nane can be fund,
  I pray you caft the Leid-lyne out;
And gif ye cannot get the Ground,
  Steir be the Compafs, keep her Rout;

Syne

Syne travers ftill, and lay about,
And gar her top twiche Wind and Waw,
    When Anker dryves, there is nae Dout
Thir tripand Tydes may tyne us a.

VIII.

Now is my pretty Pinnage ready,
    Abydand on fum Merchand Block,
But be fcho empty, be our Lady,
    Scho will be kitle of her Dok;
    Scho will refufe nae Landwart *Jok*,
Tho he fhoud fraught her for a Crown:
    Thus fair ze weil, fays gude *John Cok*,
A nobil Sailor in this Toun.

Quod SEMPLE.

The Defens of Griſſell Sandylands
For uſing of hir ſelf contrair the Ten Commands,
Being in Ward for playing of the Loun
With every ane liſt gife hir half a Croun.

I.

PErnitious People, partial in Deſpyte,
    Suſannas Juges, Sawers of Sedition,
Zour cankert Council is the Cauſe and Wyte,
    Bowſtert with Pryde, and blinded with Ambition,
    Finding nae Cryme, nor haiſing a Comiſſion
To hurt Dame *Venus* Virgins as ze do;
    Gif ze ſae raſhly rin upon Suſpition,
Ze may put others on the Pannell too.

II.

To *Sandylands* ze war ower-fair to ſchame hir,
    Sen ze with Council quietly might command hir;
Grit Fulis ze war with Fallows to defame hir,
    Haiſing nae Cauſe, but common Fame and Sklan
        der,
                        Quhen

Quhen finding no Man in the Houfe neir hand hir,
Exept a *Clerk of godly Converfation,
  Quhat gif befyde *John Duries* felf ye fand hir,
Dar ze fufpeᶜt the haly Congregation.

III.

Zour flefhly Confciens gars zou tak this Feir,
  Believe ze Virgins will be won fae fune,
Na, God forbid, but Men may bourd as neir,
  And Women be nae war, quhen that is done,
  Had fcho bene * * * *
That war a perelous Play, ane micht fufpeᶜt them,
  But Lads and Laffes will meit after None,
When *Dick* and *Durie* baith dow not correᶜt them.

IV.

Sen Drunkards, Gluttons and contentious Men,
  Scheders of Blude, and Subjeᶜts given to Greid,
May not poffefs, or Heavens high Hall get ben,
  As in the Byble daylie we may reid:

Let

---

* The Miniſter, *Beaton.*

Had fcho bene * * * * In fuch Places as are fo fullied or torn in our old Copies, that they cannot be read, we chufe rather to leave a Blank than fill them up, tho' they might be fupplied with fmall Difficulty.

Let thir be weyd alyke, till every Leid,
Syne Fornication placit amang the laif,
    Exempt zour felves throu all the Toun in Deid,
Then luke how mony zou unmarkid haif.

V.

GIF ye belife not *Betoun* be his Word,
    In hir Defens, it cannot be refufit ;
Let him that follows fecht it with the fword,
    Ane auntient Law quhen Ladyis are accufit.
    Are Minifters fic Men to be abufit,
That knaw the Scripture and the Ten Commands?
    Tho he and fcho wer in a Houfe inclufit,
That fays not he fell foul on *Sandylands.*

VI.

As for the reft, I knaw not thair Vocation,
    Thair Lyfe and Manners; but I heir Folk name
Catholick Virgins of the Congregation,   [them
    Syne were to tyne them, if ze wald obtein them:
    Quhat can ze fay, exept that ze haid fein them
With *rem in re* all nakit, bot Adherance;
    Then tak a Bow-ftring, draw it down betwein them,
And gif it fticks, that has an ill Appeirance.

                VII. ZE

VII.

Ze cative Clerks, that Colege ze frequentit
　Quhen ze were Wanflers of the wanton Band,
Now ze are laimt frae Labour, I lamment it,
　Zour Piftols tuimt, and Backfprent like a Wand,
　Snap Wark, Adieu frae * * *
And warfe than that, ze want zour pryming Powder;
　Then confciens cums with crukit Staff in Hand,
Greitand for bygane bowing Back and Shouder.

VIII.

Remember firft zour former Quality,
　And wrak nae Virgins with zour wilfull Weir;
But gif ze do, then our Regality
　Has Power plainly then to replege them heir,
　Micht they win to the Girth, I tak nae Feir,
Doun by the *Canno-Croce* I pray zou fend them,
　Where *Bannatyn* has promift to compeir,
With lawfull Reafon ready to defend them.

IX. Ane

---

* Mr. *Patrick.*

IX.

Ane Cauſe there is, thay cannot be convick,
　Ze had nae Power after the Sun was ſet.
The Provoſt gave nae Charge to *Gilbert Dick;*
　The ſpecial Thing that ſould not bein forzet,
　They were not Thieves, nor yet condemt in Dett,
Nor Red-hand tane, then was nae Cauſe ze knaw,
　* But ze let Rukes and Gleds rin throu the Nett,
And ſaikleſs Daws make ſubject to the Law.

X.

Zour partial Juge we may declyne him to,
　But ſet me doun the Parſon *Pennycuik,*
Or *Sanders Guthrie* ſee quhat he can do:
　He kens the Law, and keeps zour ain Court-
　　Buke:
　For Men of Law, I wait not quhere to luke:
James Banantyne was anes a Man of Skill;
　And gif he comes not there, I wiſh we tuke,
To keip our Dyet, Mes *David Makgill.*

　　　　　　　　　　　　XI. Quhat

* —— Little Villains muſt ſubmit to Fate,
　That great Ones may enjoy the World in State.

XI.

QUHAT Kimmer cafts the formeft Stane, lets fe,
    At thae poor Queans, ze wrangfully fufpeck
For fklenting Bouts; now better war let be,
    Than to begin and get zour felves a Geck,
    The greateft Falt I find in this Effect;
They baith tuke Pay, and put themfelves in Schame;
    But quhen the Court cums to the Town, quhat
We fall reftore them to their Stock again.   [Reck,

XII.

IN zour Tolbuith fic Prifoners to plant,
    Will be receivd richt weil, ye may confider,
Gude Captane *Adam* will not let them want
    Bedding, howbeid they fould lig all togidder.
    As for his Wife, I wald ye fould forbid her,
Hir Eyndling Toits, I true ther be nae Danger,
    Becaufe his Back is larbour groun and lidder,
Bot Underftanding now to treit a Stranger.

XIII.

THE greateft Greif I find, ze haif defamed
    Thir Luvers leil, and done their Friends but Lack,
Becaufe thair Bands were juft to be proclaimd,
    Partys had met, and made a fair Contrack:
                                    But

But now alas the Men are loppen back;
For oppen Sklander callt a fpeikand Deil,
   In grit Affairs ze had not bein fae fnack,
About the ruleing of the Common-weil.

XIV.

To punifh Part is Partiality,
   To punifh all is hard to do indeid;
But fend them heir to our Regality,
   And we fall fee gif we can ferve their Neid;
   This rural Ryme whaever likes to reid,
To *Dick* and *Dury* 'tis directed plain,
   Quhere I offend them in my Landwart Leid,
I fall be ready to reform again.

Quod SEMPLE.

THE

The Battle of *Harlaw*,

Foughten upon Friday, July 24, 1411,
againſt Donald *of the* Iſles.

I.

F RAE *Dunideir* as I cam throuch,
    Doun by the Hill of *Banochie*,
Allangſt the Lands of *Garioch*;
    Grit Pitie was to heir and ſe
The Noys and duleſum Hermonie,
That evir that dreiry Day did daw,
    Cryand the *Corynoch* on hie,
Alas! alas! for the *Harlaw*.

II.

I marvlit quhat the Matter meint,
    All Folks war in a fiery fairy:
I wiſt nocht quha was Fae or Freind;
    Zit quietly I did me carrie.

                      But

But fen the Days of auld King *Hairy*
Sic Slauchter was not hard nor fene,
 And thair I had nae Tyme to tairy,
For Biffinefs in *Aberdene*.

III.

THUS as I walkit on the Way,
 To *Inverury* as I went,
I met a Man and bad him ftay,
 Requeifting him to mak me quaint,
 Of the Beginning and the Event,
That happenit thair at the *Harlaw;*
 Then he entreited me tak tent,
And he the Truth fould to me fchaw.

IV.

Grit *Donald* of the *Yles* did claim,
 Unto the Lands of *Rofs* fum Richt,
And to the *Governour* he came,
 Them for to haif gif that he micht:

Quha

Governor, Robert Duke of *Albany*, Uncle to King *James* I. The
Account of this famous Battle may be feen in our *Scots* Hiftories.

Quha faw his Intereft was but flicht;
And thairfore anfwerit with Difdain;
 He haftit hame baith Day and Nicht,
And fent nae Bodward back again.

V.

BUT *Donald* richt impatient
 Of that Anfwer Duke *Robert* gaif,
He vowd to GOD Omnipotent,
 All the hale Lands of *Rofs* to haif,
 Or ells be graithed in his Graif.
He wald not quat his Richt for nocht.
 Nor be abufit lyk a Slaif,
That Bargin fould be deirly bocht.

VI.

THEN haiftylie he did command,
 That all his Weir-Men fhould convene,
Ilk an well harnifit frae Hand,
 To meit and heir quhat he did mein;
 He waxit wrath and vowit Tein,
Sweirand he wald furpryfe the North,
 Subdew the Burgh of *Aberdene*,
Mearns, *Angus*, and all *Fyfe*, to *Forth*.
VII. THUS

VII.

Thus with the Weir-men of the *Yles*,
  Quha war ay at his bidding bown,
With Money maid, with Forſs and Wyls,
  Richt far and neir baith up and doun:
  Throw Mount and Muir, frae Town to Town,
Allangſt the Land of *Roſs* he roars,
  And all obey'd at his Bandown,
Evin frae the *North* to *Suthren* Shoars.

VIII.

Then all the Countrie Men did zield;
  For nae reſiſtans durſt they mak,
Nor offer Battill in the Feild,
  Be forſs of Arms to beir him bak;
  Syne they reſolvit all and ſpak,
That beſt it was for thair Behoif,
  They ſould him for thair Chiftain tak,
Believing weil he did them luve.

IX.

Then he a Proclamation maid
  All Men to meet at *Inverneſs*,
Throw *Murray* Land to mak a Raid,
  Frae *Arthurſyre* unto *Spey-neſs*.

And

G

And further mair, he fent Exprefs,
To fchaw his Collours and Enfenzie,
To all and findry, mair and lefs,
Throchout the Boundis of *Boyn* and *Enzie*.

X.

AND then throw fair *Strathbogie* Land,
His Purpofe was for to purfew,
And quhafoevir durft gainftand,
That Race they fhould full fairly rew.
Then he bad all his Men be trew,
And him defend by Forfs and Slicht,
And promift them Rewardis anew,
And mak them Men of mekle Micht.

XI.

WITHOUT Refiftans as he faid,
Throw all thefe Parts he ftoutly paft,
Quhair fum war wae, and fum war glaid,
But *Garioch* was all agaft.
Throw all thefe Feilds he fped him faft,
For fic a Sicht was never fene;
And then, forfuith, he langd at laft
To fe the Bruch of *Aberdene*.

XII. To

XII.

To hinder this prowd Enterprife,
   The ftout and michty Erle of *MARR*
With all his Men in Arms did ryfe,
   Even frae *Curgarf* to *Craigyvar*,
   And down the fyde of *Don* richt far,
Angus and *Mearns* did all convene
   To fecht, or *DONALD* came fae nar
The Ryall Bruch of *Aberdene.*

XIII.

AND thus the Martial Erle of *MARR*,
   Marcht with his Men in richt Array,
Befoir the Enemie was aware,
   His Banner bauldly did difplay.
   For weil enewch they kend the Way,
And all thair Semblance weil they faw,
   Without all Dangir, or Delay,
Came haiftily to the *HARLAW.*
              XIV. WITH

MARR, Alexander Earl of *Mar*, Son of *Alexander* the Governour's
Brother.

XIV.

With him the braif Lord *OGILVY*,
  Of *Angus* Sherriff-principall,
The Conſtabill of gude *Dunde*,
  The Vanguard led before them all.
  Suppoſe in Number they war ſmall,
Thay firſt richt bauldlie did purſew,
  And maid thair Faes befoir them fall,
Quha then that Race did ſairly rew.

XV.

And then the worthy Lord *SALTON*,
  The ſtrong undoubted Laird of *DRUM*,
The ſtalwart Laird of *Lawriſtone*,
  With ilk thair Forces all and ſum.
  PANMUIR with all his Men did cum,
The Provoſt of braif *Aberdene*,
  With Trumpets and with Tuick of Drum,
Came ſchortly in thair Armour ſchene.

XVI.

These with the Erle of *MARR* came on,
  In the Reir-ward richt orderlie,
Thair Enemies to ſett upon;
  In awfull Manner hardily,

Togither

Togither vowit to live and die,
Since they had marchit mony Mylis
    For to fupprefs the Tyrannie
Of douted *DONALD* of the *Yles*.

XVII.

But he in Number Ten to Ane,
    Richt fubtilie alang did ryde,
With *Malcomtofch* and fell *Maclean*,
    With all thair Power at thair Syde,
    Prefumeand on thair Strenth and Pryde,
Without all Feir or ony Aw,
    Richt bauldlie Battill did abyde,
Hard by the Town of fair *HARLAW*.

XVIII.

The Armies met, the Trumpet founds,
    The dandring Drums alloud did touk,
Baith Armies byding on the Bounds,
    Till ane of them the Feild fould bruik.
    Nae Help was thairfor, nane wald jouk,
Ferfs was the Fecht on ilka Syde,
    And on the Ground lay mony a Bouk
Of them that thair did Battill byd.

XIX. With

XIX.

WITH doutfum Victorie they dealt,
  The bludy Battill laftit lang,
Each Man his Nibours Forfs thair felt;
  The weakeft aft-tymes gat the Wrang:
  Thair was nae Mowis thair them amang,
Naithing was hard but heavy Knocks,
  That Eccho maid a dulefull Sang,
Thairto refounding frae the Rocks.

XX.

BUT *Donalds* Men at laft gaif back;
  For they war all out of Array.
The Earl of MARRIS Men throw them brak,
  Purfewing fhairply in thair Way,
  Thair Enemys to tak or flay,
Be Dynt of Forfs to gar them yield,
  Quha war richt blyth to win away,
And fae for Feirdnefs tint the Feild.

XXI.

THEN *Donald* fled, and that full faft, .
  To Mountains hich for all his Micht;
For he and his war all agaft,
  And ran till they war out of Sicht;

And ·

And fae of *Rofs* he loft his Richt,
Thocht mony Men with him he brocht,
 Towards the *Yles* fled Day and Nicht,
And all he wan was deirlie bocht.

XXII.

THIS is (quod he) the richt Report
 Of all that I did heir and knaw,
Thocht my Difcourfe be fumthing fchort,
 Tak this to be a richt futhe Saw:
 Contrairie GOD and the Kings Law,
Thair was fpilt mekle Chriftian Blude,
 Into the Battill of *Harlaw;*
This is the Sum, fae I conclude.

XXIII.

BUT zit a bony Quhyle abyde,
 And I fall mak thee cleirly ken
Quhat Slauchter was on ilkay Syde,
 Of *Lowland* and of *Highland* Men,
 Quha for thair awin haif evir bene:
Thefe lazie Lowns micht weil be fpaird,
 Cheffit lyke Deirs into thair Dens,
And gat thair Waiges for Rewaird.

XXIV. MAL-

XXIV.

MALCOMTOSH of the Clan Heid Cheif,
  Macklean with his grit hauchty Heid,
With all thair Succour and Releif,
  War dulefully dung to the Deid:
  And now we are freid of thair Feid,
They will not lang to cum again;
  Thoufands with them without Remeid,
On *Donalds* Syd that Day war flain.

XXV.

AND on the uther Syde war loft,
  Into the Feild that difmal Day,
Chief Men of Worth (of mekle Coft)
  To be lamentit fair for ay.
  The Lord *Saltoun* of *Rothemay*,
A Man of Micht and mekle Main;
  Grit Dolour was for his Decay,
That fae unhappylie was flain.

XXVI.

OF the beft Men amang them was,
  The gracious gude Lord *OGILVY*,
The Sheriff-principal of *Angus;*
  Renownit for Truth and Equitie,

For

For Faith and Magnanimitie;
He had few Fallows in the Field,
 Zit fell by fatall Deftinie,
For he nae ways wad grant to zield.

XXVII.

SIR *James Scrimgeor* of *Duddap*, Knicht,
 Grit Conftabill of fair *Dunde*,
Unto the dulefull Deith was dicht,
 The Kingis cheif Banner-man was he,
 A valziant Man of Chevalrie,
Quhais Predeceffors wan that Place
 At *Spey*, with gude King *WILLIAM* frie,
Gainft *Murray* and *Macduncans* Race.

XXVIII.

GUDE Sir *Allexander Irving*,
 The much renownit Laird of *Drum*,
Nane in his Days was bettir fene,
 Quhen they war femblit all and fum;
 To praife him we fould not be dumm,
For Valour, Witt and Worthynefs,
 To end his Days he ther did cum,
Quhois Ranfom is remeidylefs.

XXIX. AND

XXIX.

AND thair the Knicht of *Lawriston*
    Was flain into his Armour fchene,
And gude Sir *Robert Davidfon*,
    Quha Proveft was of *Aberdene*,
    The Knicht of *Panmure*, as was fene,
A mortall Man in Armour bricht,
    Sir *Thomas Murray* ftout and kene,
Left to the Warld thair laft gude Nicht.

XXX.

THAIR was not fen King *Keneths* Days
    Sic ftrange inteftine crewel Stryf
In *Scotland* fene, as ilk Man fays,
    Quhair mony liklie loft thair Lyfe;
    Quhilk maid Divorce twene Man and Wyfe,
And mony Childrene fatherlefs,
    Quhilk in this Realme has bene full ryfe;
LORD help thefe Lands, our Wrangs redrefs.

XXXI.

IN *July*, on Saint *James* his Even,
    That Four and twenty difmall Day,
Twelve hundred, ten Score and eleven
    Of Zeirs fen CHRYST, the Suthe to fay:
    Men will remember as they may,
Quhen thus the Veritie they knaw,
    And mony a ane may murn for ay,
The brim Battil of the *Harlaw*.

                                            Ane

Ane BALLAT of the fenziet Frier of Tungland,
How he fell in the Myre fleand to Turkland.

I.

AS zung *Auror* with Chryftal Hail,
    In Orient fchewd hir Vifage pail,
A fwenyng Swyth did me affail,
    Of Sonis of Sathanis Seid;
Methocht a *Turk* of *Tartary*,
Come throw the Bounds of *Barbary*,
And lay forloppin in *Lombardy*
    Full lang, in Watchmans Weid.

II. FRAE

An Account of this Friar, who was an *Italian*, may be feen in Mr. *Lefly's* Hiftory. K. *James* IV. made him Abbot of *Tungland:* He pretended and attempted to make Gold out of other Mettals; but failing of that, he next gave out, That he could fly, and very boldly appointed the Day and Place, which was from *Stirling*-Caftle, where the King and many Spectators faw him throw himfelf with his large Wings from the Rock, and break his Thigh-bone.

II.

FRAE baptaſing for to eſchew,
Thair a religious Man he ſlew,
And cled him in his Habeit new,
    For he couth wryte and reid.
Quhen kend was his Diſſimulance,
And all his curſit Governance;
For Feir he fled, and come in *France*,
    With litill *Lombard* Leid.

III.

To be a Leiche he fenyt him thair,
Quhilk mony micht rew evirmair,
For he left nowthir ſick nor ſair
    Unſlane, or he hyne zed:
Vane-Organs he full cleinly carvit,
Quhen of his Straik ſae mony ſtarvit,
Dreid he had got quhat he deſarvit,
    He fled away gude Speid.

IV.

IN *Scotland* then the narreſt Way
He come, his Cunning till aſſay;
To ſum Men thair it was nae Play,
    The preiving of his Sciens.

In

In Pottingrie he wrocht grit Pyne,
He murdreift mony in Medecyne,
The *Jew* was of a grit Engyne,
    And generit was of Gyans.

V.

In Leich-craft he was homecyd,
He wald haif for a Nicht to byd,
A Haiknay and the Hurtmans Hyd,
    Sae mekle he was of Myance.
His Yrons was rude as ony Rawchter,
Quhair he leit Blude, it was nae Lauchter;
Full mony an Inftrument for Slauchter
    Was in his Gardevyance.

VI.

He couth gif Cure for Laxatyve,
To gar a wicht Horfe want his Lyfe,
Quha eir affay wald Man or Wyfe,
    Thair Hipps zied hiddy-giddy.
His Practicks neir war put to Preif,
Bot fudden Deid or grit Mifchief;
He had Purgation to mak a Thief
    To die without a Widdy.

                VII. Unto

VII.

UNTO nae Mefs eir preft this Prelat,
For Sound of facring Bell nor Skellat,
As Blackfmyth brukit was his Pallat,
    For batting at the Study.
Thocht he come hame a new maid Channoun.
He had difpenfit with *Matynis* Cannoun
On him come nowdir Stole nor Fannoun, .
    For fmuking of the Smydy.

VIII.

METHOCHT feir Faffonis he affailziet
To mak the Quinteffance, and failziet;
And when he faw that nocht availziet,
    A Fedrem on he tuke:
And fchupe in *Turkie* for to flie,
And quhen that he did mont on hie,
All Fowl ferliet quhat he fould be,
    That did upon him luke.

IX.

SUM held he had bene *Dedalus*,
Sum the *Minatour* marvellous,
And fum the Smyth of *Mars, Vulcanus,*
    And fum *Saturnus* Kuke.

                          And

And ay the Cufchetts at him tuggit,
The Ruiks him rent, the Ravyns druggit;
The hudit Craws his Hair furth ruggit,
 The Hevin he micht not bruke.

X.

THE Mytane and Saint *Martyns* Fowl
Wend he had bene the hornit Howle;
They fet upon him with a Zowle,
 And gaif him Dynt for Dynt.
The Golk, the Gormaw, and the Gled,
Beft him with Buffets till he bled;
The Spar-halk to the Spring him fped,
 As ferfs as Fyre off Flint.

XI.

THE Tarfall gaif him Tug for Tug,
A Stanchell hang in ilka Lug,
The Pyot furth his Pens did rug,
 The Stork ftraik ay bot Stynt.
The Biffart biffy bot Rebuke,
Scho was fae cleverous of her Cluke,
His B——s he micht nae langer bruke,
 Scho held them at a Hynt.

XII. THICK

XII.

THICK was the Cloud of Kayis and Crawis,
Of Marlzeons, Mittains, and of Mawis,
That bikkirt at his Baird with Blawis,
    In Battill him about.
They nybillt him with dinſome Cry,
The Rerd of them raiſe to the Sky,
And evir he cryd on Fortune, Fy,
    His Lyfe was into Dowt.

XIII.

THE Jae him ſkrippit with a Skryke,
And ſkornit him as it was lyk,
The Egill ſtrong at him did ſtryk,
    And rawcht him mony a Rout.
For Feir uncunnandly he cawkit,
Quhyle all his Penns wer drownt and drawkit,
He maid a hundreth Nolt all hawkit,
    Beneath him with a Spowt.

XIV.

HE ſchure his Feddreme that was ſchene,
And ſlippit out of it full clene,
And in a Myre, up to the Ene,
    Amang the Glar did glyd.

                                The

The Fowlis all at the Fedreme dang,
As at a Monſter, them amang,
Quhyle all the Penns of it outſprang
    Intill the Air full wyde.

XV.

AND he lay at the Plunge eirmair,
Sae langs he hard a Ravin rair;
The Craws him ſocht with Crys of Cair
    In every Schaw beſyde.
Had he reveild bene to the Ruiks,
They had him riven with thair Cluiks:
Thre Days in Dubs amang the Duiks,
    He did with Dirt him hyde.

XVI.

THE Air was dirkint with the Fowls,
That came with Zawmers and with Zowls,
With Skryking, Skryming, and with Scouls
    To tak him in the Tyde.
I walknit with the Noyſs and Schout,
Sic hydious Beir was me about,
Senſyne I curſt that cankirt Rout,
    Quaireir I gang or ryde.

Finis quod DUNBAR.

Tyd-

H

TYDINGS frae the SESSION.

I.

A MURELANDS Man of Uplands Mak,
    At Hame thus to his Nychbour ſpak,
What Tydings, Goſſip, Peice or Weir?
The tother rounit in his Eir,
    I tell zou this under Confeſſion,
But laitly lichtit aff my Meir,
    I come of *Edinburgh* frae the Seſſion.

II.

QUHAT Tydings hard ze thair, I pray zou?
The tother anſwert, I ſall ſay zou,
Keip this all ſecreit, gentil Brothir,
Is nae Man thair that treſts ane uther:
    A common Doer of Tranſgreſſion,
Of Innocents preveins a Futher:
    Sic Tydings hard I at the Seſſion.

III. SUM

III.

Sum with his Maik, rowns him to pleis,
That envyous wald byt aff his Neis;
His Fae him by the Oxter leids;
Sum Patters with his Mouth on Beids,
    That has his Mynd all on Oppreſſion:
Sum becks full law, and ſchaws bair Heids,
    Wald luke full heich war not the Seſſion.

IV.

Sum bydand Law, lays Land in Wed;
Sum ſuperexpendit gaes to Bed,
Sum ſpeids, cauſe he in Court has Meins,
Sum of Partiality compleins,
    How Feid and Favour fleims Diſcretion:
Sum ſpeiks full fair and falſly feins;
    Sic Things I hard and ſaw at Seſſion.

V.

Sum Summonds caſts, and ſum excepts,
Sum ſtand befyd and ſkaild Law kepps;
Sum is delayd, ſum wins, ſum tynes;
Sum maks him merry at the Wynes;
    Sum is put out of his Poſſeſſion;
Sum herrit, and on Credance dynes;
    Sic Tydings hard I at the Seſſion.

VI. Sum

VI.

Sum ſweirs, and gaes clein up with GOD,
Sum in a Lamb-ſkin is a Tod,   .
Sum in his Tung his Kindneſs turſes,
Sum cuts at Throats, and ſum pyks Purſes:
     Sum gaes to Gallows with Proceſſion;
Sum ſains the Seit, and ſum them curſes;
     Sic Tydings hard I at the Seſſion.

VII.

Religious Men of divers Places,
Cum thair to wou, and ſee fair Faces,
Baith *Carmelites* and *Cordiliers*,
To Gemer cum, and get mae Friers,
     Unmindful of thair cheſt Profeſſion,
The zunger at the elder leirs;
     Sic Tydings hard I at the Seſſion.

VIII.

Thair cums zung Monks of hie Complexion,
Of Mynd devote, Luve and Affection;
And in the Court thair het Fleſh dant,
Full Father-lyk, with Pech and Pant:
     They are ſae humble of Interceſſion,
Thair Errand all kynd Women grant:
     Sic Tydings hard I at the Seſſion.

                          IX. Sum

IX.

Sum honeſt Lords adorn the Bench,
Sum mynds nocht but his Wine and Wench;
Sum has Law Learning of his awin,
Sum wants and lippens to his Man,
    In ilka Cauſe to get a Leſſon;
Sum cankirt girns, be Party thrawin,
    And fleims fair Juſtice frae the Seſſion.

X.

The Advocates I may nocht wyte,
Nor yet the Lads that Lybalds wryte;
For its thair Craft, and they maun fen,
This has nae Spevie in his Pen,
    Nor that a Palſie in Expreſſion;
But weil I wate an of ilk Ten,
    Micht very weil gane all the Seſſion.

Quod Dunbar.

A

A

Generall SATYRE.

I.

DEvorit with Dreim devifing in my Slumber,
How that this Realm with Nobles out of
Number,
Gydit, provydit fae mony Years has bene;
And now fic Hunger, fic Cowarts, and fic Cumber,
Within this Land was nevir hard nor fene.

II.

Sic Pryd with Prelats, fae few to preich and pray;
Sic hunt of Harlots, with them baith Nicht and Day,
They that fould have ay thair God afore thair Ene,
Sae nyce in Array, fae ftrange to thair Abay,
Within this Land was nevir hard or fene.

III. Sae

III.

SAE mony Preifts cled up in fecular Weid,
With blafing Breifts, cafting thair Clais abreid;
 It is no Neid to tell of quhome I mein,
To quhome the Creid and Teftament to reid
 Within this Land was nevir hard nor fene.

IV.

SAE mony Maifters, fae mony gowckit Clerks,
Sae mony Waifters, to GOD and all His Warks,
 Sic fyrie Sparks, difpytful frae the Splene,
Sic lofin Sarks, fae mony Glengore Marks,
 Within, &c.

V.

SAE mony Lords, fae mony naturale Fules,
That better accords, to play them at the Trules,
 Nor feis the Dules, that commons did fuftene.
New tane frae Schules, fae mony Anis and Mules,
 Within, &c.

VI.

SAE meikle Treaffon, fae mony partial Saws,
Sae little Reafon, to help the common Caufe,
 That all the Laws are not fet by ane Bene,
Sic fenziet Flaws, fae mony waftit Waws,
 Within, &c.

VII. SAE

VII.

Sae mony Theivs and Murderers weil kend,
Sae grit Releivs of Lords them till deffend,
 Becaufe they fpend the Pelf them betwene,
Sae few till wend this Mifcheif till amend,
 Within, &c.

VIII.

This to correct, they fhore with mony Cracks,
But fmall the Effect of Speir or bartar Ax, [kein,
 Quhen Courage lacks, that fuld the Corfs mak
Sae mony Jacks, and Brats on Beggars Baks,
 Within, &c.

IX.

Sic Vant of Wouftours, with Hearts in finful Satures,
Sic brawland Bofters, degenerate frae thair Natures,
 And fic Regratours, the pure Man to prevene;
Sae mony Traytors, fae mony Rubeators,
 Within, &c.

X.

Sae mony Juges, and Lords new made of late,
Sae fmall Refuges, the pure Man to debate;
 Sae mony Eftate, for common Weil fae quhene,
Owre all the Gate, fae mony Theives fa tait,
 Within, &c.

XI. Sae

XI.

SAE mony a Sentance retreitit for to win
Geir and Aquentance, or Kyndnefs of thair Kin;
   Thay think nae Sin, quhair Proffit cums betwene
Sae mony a Gin, to haift them to the Pin,
   Within, &c.

XII.

SIC Knavis and Crakkars, to play at Cards and Dyce,
Sic Haland-Shakers, quhilk ate *Cowkelbys* Gryce,
   Ar halden of Pryce, when Lymers do convene;
Sic Store of Vyce, sae mony Witts unwyfe,
   Within, &c.

XIII.

SAE mony Merchands, fae mony ar menfworne,
Sic pure Tennands, fic curfing Ein and Morn,
   Quhilk flays the Corn, and Fruit that grows grene;
Sic Skaith and Skorn, fae mony Paitlaits worn,
   Within, &c.

XIV.

SAE mony Rackets, fae mony Ketch Pillars,
Sic Balls, fic Nackets, and fic Tutivilaris,
   And fic Ill-willars, to fpeik of King and Quene,
Sic Pudding-fillars, defcending doun frae Millars,
   Within, &c.

XV. SIC

XV.

Sɪc Fardingails on Flags as fat as Quhails,
Fattit lyk Fouls, with Hatts that nocht avails,
    And ſic foul Tails, to ſweip the Cauſy clene,
The Duſt up ſails, ſae mony with uck ſails
    Within, &c.

XVI.

Sᴀᴇ mony a Kitty, dreſt up in Golden Chenze,
Sae few witty, that weil can Fables fenze,
    With apil Renze, ay ſhawand her Golden Chene;
Of Sathans Senzie ſure ſic an unſall Menzie
    Within this Land was nevir hard nor ſene.

Quod Dᴜɴʙᴀʀ.

Wiſe

Wise SAYINGS.

———•❊•———

IT that I gife, I haif,
   It that I len, I craif,
It that I fpend, is myne,
It that I leif, I tyne:
  Get and faif, and thou falt haif,
  Len and grant, and thou falt want;
Wha in his Plenty taks not Heid,
He fall haif Falt in Tyme of Neid:
    When eir I lend,
    I am a Friend,
    And whan I craif,
    I am unkynd;
Thus of my Friend, I mak a Fae,
I fhrew me, gif I mair do fae.

A zung Man Chiftane, wittles,
A pure Man Spendar, gettles,
Ane auld Man Trechour, truthlefs,
A Woman Lowpar, landlefs;
   Be gude Saint *Giel*,
Sall nevir ane of thir do weil.

             THE

THE

COMPLAINT.

An EPISTLE to his Miſtreſs
on the Force of LUVE.

I.

QUHAIR Luve is kendlit comfortleſs,
    Ther is nae Fever half ſae fell,
Frae *Cupid* keiſt his Dart begeſs,
    I had nae Hap to ſaif my ſell,
    Lyk as my wofull Heart can tell,
My inwart Pains and Siching ſair;
    For weil I wat the Pains of Hell
Unto my Pain can nocht compair.

II. For

II.

For ony Malledy, ze ken,
  Except peuir Luve, or than ſtark Deid,
Help may be had frae Hands of Men,
  Throw Medicines to mak Remeid:
  For Harms of Body, Hands or Heid,
The Pottingars will purge the Pains;
  But all the Members are at Feid,
Quhair that the Law of Luve remains.

III.

As *Tantalus* in Watter ſtands,
  To ſtanche his thriſty Appetyte,
Bewailing Body, Heid and Hands,
  The River fleis him in Diſpyte;
  Sae does my luſty Lady qwhyte,
She fleis the Place where I repair:
  To hungry Men is ſmal Delyte
To twitch the Meit, and eit nae mair.

IV.

The nar the Flame, the hetter Fyre,
  The mair I pyne, zet I perſew,
The mair enkindlis my Diſyre,
  Frae I behald her heavenly Hew;

Pure

Pure *Piramus* himſelf he ſlew,
Made Saul and Body to diſſaver,
   He diet but anes, farwel, adiew,
I daylie die, and zet dies never.

V.

ZIT *Jaſon* did enjoy *Medea*,
   And *Theſeus* gat his *Adriane*,
Dido diſſaved was with *Enea*,
   And *Demophoy* his Lady wan;
   Gif Women trowd ſic Traytors than,
For till enjoy the Fruits of Luve,
   Quhy wald ze ſlay zour ſaikles Man,
Quha never mynds for to remuve.

VI.

THOCHT ferſs *Achil*, that worthie Knicht,
   Was ſlain for Luve, the Suthe to ſay,
Leander on a ſtormy Nicht
   Diet fleitand on the Billous gray;
   Thocht *Troyalus* he langourt ay,
Still waitand for his Luves Return,
   Had not ſic Pyne (thairs was but Play)
As daylie does my Body burn.

                VII. As

VII.

As Pol to Pylatts does appeir
 Far brichtar than the Stars about,
Sae does zour Viſage ſhine as cleir
 As Roſe amang the raſkal Rout;
 War *Paris* leivand now, bot Dout,
And had the Golden Ball to ſerve,
 I wate he wald ſune wail zou out,
And leif baith *Venus* and *Minerve.*

VIII.

Now Paper pas, and at her ſpeir,
 Gif pleiſe her Prudeñce to imprint it?
My faithfull Heart I ſend it heir,
 In Signe of Paper I preſent it;
 Wad GOD my Body war fornent it,
That I micht ſerve hir Grace bot Glammer,
 To be hir Knaif I am contentit,
Or ſmalleſt Varlet of hir Chammer.

Quod King HENRY STEWART.

CUPID

Cupid quareld for his Tyrannie,
Blindnes and Injuſtice.

I.

QUHOME ſould I wyt for my Miſchance,
　　But *Cupid* King of Variance,
Thy Court, without Conſiderance,
　　　　Quhen I it knew,
Or evir made the Obſervance,
　　　　Richt fair I rew.

II.

THOU and thy Law ar Inſtruments
Of diverſs Inconveniments;
Thy Service mony ſair repents,
　　　　Knawing the Quarrell,
Quhen Body, Fame and Subſtance ſhents,
　　　　And Saul in Perel.

III. QUHAT

III.

QUHAT is thy Manrent but Mifcheif,
Sturt, Anger, Grunching, Yre and Greif,
Ill Lyfe, and Langour bot Releife,
  Of wounds fae wan,
Difplifour, Pain, and hie Repreife
  Of GOD and Man.

IV.

THOU luves all them that loudeft leis,
And follows fafteft them that fleis;
Thou lichtlies all trew Properties
  Of Luve exprefs,
And marks quhen neir a Styme thou feis,
  And hits begefs.

V.

BLIND Buk! but at the Bound thou fhutes,
And them forbeirs that thee rebutes;
Thou ryves thair Hearts ay frae the Rutes,
  Quilk ar thy awin,
And cures them that cares not three Cutes
  To be mifknawn.

VI. THOU

I

VI.

Thou art in Friendſhip with thy Fae,
And to thy beſt Friends fremit ay,
Thou fleims all faithful Men thee frae,
        Of ſtedfaſt Thocht,
Regarding nane but them perfay
        That cures the nocht.

VII.

Thou chirrieſs them that with thee chyds,
And bannieſs them with thee abyds:
Thou hes thy Horn ay in thair Syds
        That cannot flie;
Thay furder warſt in thee confyds,
        I ſay for me.

Quod Alexr. Scot.

THE

THE

Auld Mans inveighing againſt Mouth-Thanklefs.

I.

A NE agit Man twyce Forty Zeirs,
 After the haly Days of *Zule*,
I hard him carp amang the Freirs,
 Of Order gray, makand grit Dule,
 Richt as he war a furious Fule;
Aft-tymes he ficht, and faid Alace!
 Be *Claud* my Care may nevir cule,
That I fervt evir *Mouth-thanklefs*.

II.

THROCH Ignorance, and Folly, Zouth,
 My Preterit Tyme I wald neir fpair,
Plefance to put into that Mouth,
 Till Aige faid, Fule, let be thy Fare,

       And

And now my Heid is quhyt and liair,.
For feiding of that fowmart Face,
   Quhairfor I murn baith late and air,
That I fervt evir *Mouth-thanklefs*.

III.

SILVER and Gold that I micht get
   Beifands, Brotches, Robes and Rings,
Frelie to gife, I wald nocht let,
   To pleife the Mulls attour all Things.
   Right as the Swan for Sorrow fings,
Before her Deid a little Space,
   Richt fae do I, and my Hands wrings,
That I fervt evir *Mouth-thanklefs*.

IV.

BETTIR it were a Man to ferve
   With Honour brave beneath a Sheild,
Nor her to pleis, thocht thou fould fterve,
   That will not luke on thee in Eild,
   Frae that thou has nae Hair to heild
Thy Heid frae harming that it hes,
   Quhen *Pen* and Purfe and all ar peild,
Tak then a Meis of *Mouth-thanklefs*.

V. IT

V.

IT may be in Example ſene,
  The Grund of Truth wha underſtude,
* Frae in thy Bag thou beirs thyne Een,
  Thou gets nae Grace but for thy Gude,
  At *Venus* Cloſet, to conclude,
Call ze not this a cankert Caſe:
  Now GOD help and the haly Rude,
And keip all Men frae *Mouth-thankleſs.*

VI.

O brukil Zouth in Tyme behald,
  And in thy Heart thir Words gae graif,
Or thy Complexion gather Cauld,
  Amend thy Miſs, thy ſelf to ſaif,
  The Bliſs abune gif thou wald haif,
And of thy Gilt Remit and Grace.
  All this I hard an auld Man raif,
After the Zule, of *Mouth-thankleſs.*

Quod KENNEDY.

---

* Makes use of Speŏacles.

THE

The *Soutar* defcryvit by the *Tailzior*.

I.

THou leis Loun, thou leis, thou leis,
    Zone are Soutars that thou feis,
Kneiland full lawly on thair Kneis,
    Thair Gods till adorn.
Be Saint *Girnega*, that grim Ghaift,
To hale ther Hairfneffes on haift,
Of moltin Tauch thay tak a Teft
    On *Monandays* at Morn.

II.

To hald them halefome at the Heart,
Sum of fat Uly fpews a Quart,
Uthers a Pynt for thair awn Part,
    Of foul Soutars Blek,

                        Thus

Thus fum fits, and fum fews,
Sum byts the Birs, fum Uly fpews,
And he keips ay beft his Kews,
      Spouts in his Nichbours Nek.

III.

OF Tauch or Uly when thay want,
Sir *Girnega* will give a Gant,
And bok a Pynt at ilka Pant,
      And dr— them Roset rowth.
Wald Man and Wyf all do as I,
When eir we faw them we fould cry,
Fy on them, fich! and fy! fy! fy!
      Thay fyle the Wind in trowth.

THE

THE

Soutars Anſwer to the *Tailzior*.

I.

FALSE clatterand Kenſy, Kuckold Knaif,
    Blaſphemand Baird in thy Backbyting,
Of me thou ſall an Anſwer haif,
    Fumart cum forth, and face my Flyting,
    Warſe than a Warlo in thy Wryting;
Thou Sathans Seid ay ſet to Evil,
    Mandrag, Memerkyn, miſmade Myting,
I ſall thee conjure lyk the Devil.

II.

Fy on the Tailzior never trew,
    Frae Claith weil can thou cleik a Clout,
Of Stomoks ſtown baith red and blew,
    A Bag fou anes thou bore about.

                    They

They followt thee with Cry and Shout,
Hey, hald the Thief that ſtaw the Claith;
Thou will be hangt, haif thou nae Dout,
For mony preſumptous forſworn Aith.

III.

AMANG the Wyves it ſall be witten
  Thou was ane Knakat in the Way,
For louſy Seims that thou haſt bitten,
  Thy Gumes are giltin grein and gray;
  Thy Couch is on a Sonk of Strae,
Peild Prick-louſe of a Pudding Price,
  Breik Boutcher on a Suny Brae;
Wae worth thee Wirryar of quhyt Lyce.

IV.

THOU zeid with Elwand, Sheir and Thymbill,
  Full mony a Day ſeikand thy Craft;
For Halfpenies thy Hand zeid nimble,
  Grit Blads and Bitts thou ſtaw full aft;
  Quha delt with thee thay wer full daft,
For on thy Back, as all Men kens,
  Wer broken mony a gude Ax Shaft,
For wrangus Geir of uther Mens.

V. THY

V.

THY Wyfe ſcho wont a Man ſhe gat
  Of thee, quhen that thou was weil brankit,
And ſcho gat but ane Cur Knakat,
  A foul Taid Carle, all Tailzior ſhankit,
  For Clais that thou miſmade and mankit,
Thou dar not dwell wher thou was born;
  Zet afterwart thou ſall be hankit
Betwixt *Kirkaldy* and *Kingorne.*

Quod STEWART.

BEtwix twa Tods a crawing Cok,
    Betwix twa Friers a Maid in her Smok,
  Betwix twa Cats a Mous,
  Betwix twa Tailziors a Lous;
Schaw me, gude Sir, not as a Stranger,
Quhilk of thir Fours in griteſt Danger?

ANSWER.

FOXIS ar fell at crawing Coks,
Friers are fers at Maids in thair Smoks,
Cats ar cautelus in taking Myce,
Tailziors ar Tyrrans in killing Lyce.

A

*A BALLAT made to the Scorn and
Derifion of wanton Women.*

I.

ZE lufty Ladyis, luke
　　The rackles Lyves ze leid,
Haunt nocht in Hole or Nuke,
　To hurt zour Womanheid;
　I red, for beft Remeid,
Forbeir all Place prophane;
　Gif this be Caufe of Feid,
I fall not fayt again.

II.

QUHAT is fic Luve but Luft,
　A lytill for Delyte,
To hant that Game robuft,
　And beiftly Apetyte;

I now-

I nowther fleich nor flyte,
But Veritie tell plain;
    Tak ye this in Defpyte,
I fall not fayt again.

III.

THE wyfeft Scho may fone
    Seducit be and fchent,
Syne frae the Deid be done,
    Perchance fall fair repent;
    Ower late is to lament,
Frae Belly dow not lane,
    Therfor in Tyme tak tent:
I fall not fayt again.

IV.

LICHT Wenches Luve will fawin,
    Evin lyke a *Spanzeolis* Lauchter,
To * * *
    Be them, lift Geir bechaucht hir;
    For Conzie ze may caucht hir,
To * * *
    And nevir fpeir quhais aucht hir;
I fall not fayt again.

V. THOCHT

V.

THOCHT bruckle Women hants
  In Luft to leid their Lyvis,
And Widdow Men that wants
  To fteil a Pair of Wyvis;
  But quhere that marriet Wyvis
Gaes by thair Hufbands Bane,
  That Houfhald nevir thryvis,
I fayt, and fayt again.

VI.

IT fets not Maidens als
  To let Men lowfe thair Lace,
Nor clym about Mens Hals,
  To clap, to kifs, and brace,
  Nor round in fecret Place;
Sic Treatment is a Train
  To cleave thair Quaver-Cafe,
And breid them Dule and Pain.

VII.

FAREWEIL with Cheftetie,
  Frae Wenches fall a Chucking,
Thair follows Things thre,
  To gar them gae a Gucking,
                    Imbracing,

Imbracing, Tigging, Plucking;
Thir foure the Suth to fane,
Enforfis them * * *
I fall not fayt again.

VIII.

Sum lykes new cum to Toun,
  With Jeigs to mak them joly,
Sum lykes danfs up and doun
  To miefs thair Melancholy;
  Sum lykes Sang, troly loly,
And fum of rigging fain;
  Lyk Fillocks full of Foly,
With litle Gier thair ain.

IX.

Sum Mune-brunt Maidens myld,
  At None-tyde of the Nicht,
Are chapit up with Chyld,
  Bot Coal or Candle-licht;

                                    Sua

Enforfis them * * * 'Tis not impoffible but a complete Copy of
this old Ballad may be found to fupply thefe few Blanks.

Sua fum faid, Mayds has Slicht
To play, and tak nae Pane,
  Syne fchift thair fells frae Sicht,
I fall not fayt again.

X.

SUM thinks nae Schame to clap
  And kifs in open Ways;
Sum cannot keip her ap
  Frae lanfing, as fcho lyes;
  Sum goes fae gymp in Gyfe,
Or fcho war kiffd, but plain,
  Scho leur be married thryis,
And thre Tymes thryis again.

XI.

MAIR Gentrice is to jot
  Undir a Silkin Goun,
Than with quhyt Pettycot
  And redyar ay boun,
  The denkeft foneft doun,
The faireft but refrain,
  The gayeft greateft Loun,
But dinna tellt again.

XII. THE

XII.

THE moir degeft and grave,
   The grydiar * * *
The nyceft to reffave
   Upon thair * * *
   The quhytlieft will quhipit,
And nocht thair * * *
   The lefs, the larger hippit;
I fall not fayt again.

XIII.

Lo Ladyis gif this be,
   A gude Counfale I geife zou,
To fave zour Honeftie,
   Frae Sklander to releife zou;
   But Ballats mae to breif zou,
I will not break my Brain,
   Suppofe ze fould mifcheive you,
I fall not fayt again.

                              Quod SCOTT.

On the Uncertainty of Life and Fear of Death, or a Lament for the Loſs of the Poets.

I.

OUR Pleaſance heir is all vain Glory,
 This Warld falſe but tranſatory;
The Fleſh is bruckle, the Feynd is ſlie,
 Timor mortis conturbat me.

II.

THE State of Man dois change and vary,
Now ſound, now ſeik, now blyth, now ſary,
Now danſand merry, now lyk to die,
 Timor mortis conturbat me.

III.

No State in all the Eard ſtands ſicker,
But as the Weſt-Wind wavis the wicker,
Sae wanes this warldly Vanity,
 Timor mortis, &c.

IV. DOUN

K

IV.

Doun to the Death gois all Eftates,
Princes, Prelates and Potentates,
Baith rich and pure of all Degree,
   Timor, &c.

V.

He taks the Knichts into the Feild,
Enarmed under Helm and Sheild,
He Victor is at all mellie,
   Timor, &c.

VI.

That ftrang invynfable Tyrrand
Taks, on the Muthers Breift fuckand,
The Babe, full of Benignitie,
   Timor, &c.

VII.

He taks the Campion in the Stour,
The Captain clofd within the Towir,
The Lady in Bowre, full of Bewtie,
   Timor, &c.

VIII. He

VIII.

He fpares no Lord for his Pufiance,
Nor Clerk for his Intelligence;
His awfull Strake may no Man flee,
    Timor, &c.

IX.

Art Magicians and Aftrologs,
Rethoris, Logitians, Theologs,
Get Help frae nae Conclufions flee,
    Timor, &c.

X.

In Medecyne the moft Practitians,
Leiches, Surrigians and Phefitians,
Themfelves frae Death may not fupplie,
    Timor, &c.

XI.

I fee the Makkars, mang the laif,
Plays here thair Padzians, fyne goes to Graif;
Not fpairt is thair fweit Facultie,
    Timor, &c.

                       XII. He

XII.

He has done petouſly devore,
The nobil *Chawſer* of Makkars Flowir,
The *Monk of Berry* and *Gower* all thre,
 Timor mortis conturbat me.

XIII.

The gude Sr *Hew* of *Eglintoun,*
Etrick, Heriot and *Winton,*
He has tane out of this Countrey,
 Timor, &c.

XIV.

That Scorpion fell has done infek,
Maiſter *John Clerk* and *James Affleck,*
Frae Ballat making and Tragedy,
 Timor, &c.

      XV. *Ho-*

---

* 'Tis worthy of Notice how generouſly Mr. *Dunbar* pays his Reſpeɛts to the Memory of the renowned *Chaucer, Gower* and *Lidgate,* before he names his own Country Poets.

XV.

Holand and *Barbor* he has bereft,
Allace! that he not with us left
Sr *Mungo Lockhart* of the *Lie*,
    Timor mortis conturbat me.

XVI.

Clerk of *Tranent* eik he has tane,
That made the Aventers of Sr *Gawane*,
Sr *Gilbert Gray* endit has he,
    Timor, &c.

XVII.

He has *Blind Hary* and *Sandy Trail*
Slain with his Shot of mortall Hail,
Quhilk *Patrick Johnſon* micht not flie,
    Timor, &c.

XVIII.

He has reft *Merſar* his Indyte,
That did in Luve ſo lyſlie wryte,
So ſchort, ſo quick, of Sentens hie,
    Timor, &c.

                        XIX. He

XIX.

He has tane *Rowl* of *Aberdene,*
And gentle *Rowl* of *Corftorphyne;*
Twa bettir Fallows did no Man fie,
    Timor mortis conturbat me.

XX.

In *Dumfermling* he has tane *Broun,*
With gude Mr. *Robert Henryfon;*
Sr *John the Rofs* imbraift has he,
    Timor, &c.

XXI.

And he has now tane, laft of aw,
The gentle *Stobo* and *Quintene Schaw,*
Of quhome all Wichts has grit Pitie,
    Timor, &c.

XXII.

And Mr. *Walter Kennedy*
In Poynt of Death lyes werely;
Grit Rewth it wer that fo fould be,
    Timor, &c.

XXIII. Sen

XXIII.

SEN he has all my Brethren tane,
He will not let me leive alane;
On Forſs I maun his nixt Prey be,
 Timor, &c.

XXIV.

SEN for the Death Remeid is none,
Beſt is that we for Death diſpone;
Aftir our Death, that live may we,
 Timor mortis conturbat me.

POSTSCRIPT.

XXV.

SUTHE I forſie, if Spae-craft had,
 Frae Hethir-Muirs ſall ryſe a LAD,
Aftir twa Centries pas, ſall he
 Revive our Fame and Memorie.

XXVI. THEN

XXVI.

THEN fall we flourifh EVIR GRENE;
All Thanks to carefull *Bannantyne*,
And to the *PATRON kind and frie,
    Quha lends the LAD baith them and me.

XXVII.

FAR fall we fare, baith Eift and Weft,
Owre ilka Clyme by *Scots* poffeft;
Then fen our Warks fall nevir die,
    Timor mortis non turbat me.

Quod DUNBAR.

---

* *Patron*, Mr. *William Carmichael*, Brother to the Earl of *Hyndford*,
who lent A. R. that curious MSS. collected by Mr. *George Bannan-*
tyne, *Anno* 1568, from whence thefe Poems are printed.

The

The *WIFE* *of* Auchtermuchty.

I.

IN *Auchtermuchty* dwelt a Man,
  An Huſband, as I heard it tawld,
Quha weil coud tipple out a Can,
  And nowther luvit Hungir nor Cauld,
Till anes it fell upon a Day,
  He zokit his Plewch upon the Plain;
But ſchort the Storm wald let him ſtay,
  Sair blew the Day with Wind and Rain.

II.

HE lowſd the Plewch at the Lands End,
  And draife his Owſen hame at Ene;
Quhen he came in he blinkit ben,
  And ſaw his *Wyfe* baith dry and clene,
Set beikand by a Fyre full bauld,
  Suppand fat Sowp, as I heard ſay:
The Man being weary, wet and cauld,
  Betwein thir twa it was nae Play.

III. Quod

III.

Quod he, quhair is my Horſes Corn,
   My Owſen has nae Hay nor Strae,
Dame, ye maun to the Plewch the Morn,
   I ſall be Huſſy gif I may.
This Seid-time it proves cauld and bad,
   And ze ſit warm, nae Troubles ſe;
The Morn ze ſall gae with the Lad,
   And ſyne zeil ken what Drinkers drie.

IV.

Gudeman, quod ſcho, content am I,
   To tak the Plewch my Day about,
Sae ye rule weil the Kaves and Ky,
   And all the Houſe baith in and out:
And now ſen ze haif made the Law,
   Then gyde all richt and do not break;
They ſicker raid that neir did faw,
   Therfor let naithing be negleƈt.

V.

But ſen ye will Huſſyſkep ken,
   Firſt ye maun ſift and ſyne ſall kned;
And ay as ze gang butt and ben,
   Luke that the Bairns dryt not the Bed:

                    And

And lay a faft Wyfp to the Kiln,
   We haif a dear Farm on our Heid;
And ay as ze gang forth and in,
   Keip weil the Gaiflings frae the Gled.

VI.

THE Wyfe was up richt late at Ene,
   I pray Luck gife her ill to fair,
Scho kirn'd the Kirn, and fkumt it clene,
   Left the Gudeman but bledoch bair:
Then in the Morning up fcho gat;
   And on hir Heart laid hir Disjune,
And pat as mekle in hir Lap,
   As micht haif ferd them baith at Nune.

VII.

. SAYS, *Jok*, be thou Maifter of Wark,
   And thou fall had, and I fall ka,
Ife promife thee a gude new Sark,
   Either of round Claith or of fma.
Scho lowft the Owfen aught or nyne,
   And bynt a Gad-ftaff in her Hand:
Up the *Gudeman* raife aftir fyne,
   And faw the *Wyfe* had done Command.
               VIII. HE

VIII.

HE draif the Gaiflings forth to feid,
  Thair was but fevenfum of them aw,
And by thair comes the greidy Gled,
  And lickt up five, left him but twa:
Then out he ran in all his Mane,
  How fune he hard the Gaiflings cry;
But than or he came in again,
  The Kaves brak loufe and fuckt the Ky.

IX.

THE Kaves and Ky met in the Loan,
  The Man ran with a Rung to red,
Than by cam an illwilly Roan,
  And brodit his Buttoks till they bled:
Syne up he tuke a Rok of Tow,
  And he fat down to fey the Spinning;
He loutit doun our neir the Low,
  Quod he this Wark has ill Beginning.

X.

THE Leam up throu the Lum did flow,
  The Sute tuke Fyre it flyed him than,
Sum Lumps did fall and burn his Pow;
  I wat he was a dirty Man:

Zit

Zit he gat Water in a Pan,
 Quherwith he flokend out the Fyre:
To foup the Houfe he fyne began,
 To had all richt was his Defyre.

XI.

HYND to the Kirn then did he ftoure,
 And jumblit at it till he fwat,
Quhen he had rumblit a full lang Hour,
 The Sorrow crap of Butter he gat;
Albeit nae Butter he could get,
 Zit he was cummert with the Kirn,
And fyne he het the Milk fae het,
 That ill a Spark of it wad zyrne.

XII.

THEN ben thair cam a greidy Sow,
 I trow he cund hir litle Thank:
For in fcho fhot hir mekle Mow,
 And ay fcho winkit, and ay fcho drank.
He tuke the Kirnftaff be the Schank,
 And thocht to reik the Sow a Rout,
The twa left Gaiflings gat a Clank,
 That Straik dang baith thair Harns out.

XIII. THEN

XIII.

THEN he bure Kendling to the Kill,
    But fcho ftart all up in a Low,
Quhat eir he heard what eir he faw,
    That Day he had nae Will to * *
Then he zied to take up the Bairns,
    Thocht to have fund them fair and clene;
The firft that he gat in his Arms,
    Was a bedirtin to the Ene.

XIV.

THE firft it fmelt fae fappylie,
    To touch the lave he did not grein:
The Deil cut aff thair Hands, quoth he,
    That cramd zour Kytes fae ftrute zeftrein.
He traild the foul Sheits down the Gate,
    Thocht to haif wufh them on a Stane,
The Burn was rifen grit of Spait,
    Away frae him the Sheits has tane.

XV.

THEN up he gat on a Know-heid,
    On hir to cry, on hir to fchout:
Scho hard him, and fcho hard him not,
    But ftoutly fteird the Stots about.

                        Scho

Scho draif the Day unto the Nicht,
    Scho lowſt the Plewch, and ſyne cam hame;
Scho fand all wrang that ſould bene richt,
    I trow the Man thocht mekle Schame.

XVI.

Quoth he, my Office I forſake,
    For all the hale Days of my Lyfe;
For I wald put a Houſe to Wraik,
    Had I been twenty Days Gudewyfe.
Quoth ſcho, weil mot ze bruke your Place,
    For truely I ſall neir accept it;
Quoth he, Feynd fa the Lyars Face,
    But zit ze may be blyth to get it.

XVII.

Then up ſcho gat a mekle Rung;
    And the Gudeman made to the Dore,
Quoth he, Dame, I ſall hald my Tung,
    For and we fecht I'll get the war:
Quoth he, when I forſuke my Plewch,
    I trow I but forſuke my Skill:
Then I will to my Plewch again;
    For I and this Houſe will nevir do weil.

Quod MOFFAT.

THE

The Borrowſtoun Mous, and the Land-wart Mous.

I.

E Asop relates a Tale weil worth Renown,
 Of twa wie Myce, and they war Siſters deir,
Of quhom the Elder dwelt in Borrowſtoun,
 The Zunger ſcho wond upon Land weil neir,
 Richt ſolitair beneth the Buſs and Breir,
Quhyle on the Corns and Wraith of labouring Men,
As Outlaws do, ſcho maid an eaſy Fen.

II.

THE Rural Mous, unto the Winter-tyde,
 Thold Cauld and Hunger aft, and grit Diſtreſs:
The uther Mous that in the Burgh can byde,
 Was Gilt-bruther, and made a frie Burges,
 Tol frie, and without Cuſtom mair or leſs,
And Friedom had to gae quhair eir ſcho liſt,
Amang the Cheis and Meil in Ark or Kiſt.

III. ANE

III.

ANE Tyme when ſcho was full, and on Fute fair,
   Scho tuke in Mynd her Siſter up-on-Land,
And langt to ken her Weilfair and her Cheir,
   And ſe quhat Lyf ſcho led under the Wand:
   Bare-fute alane, with Pykſtaff in her Hand,
As Pilgrim pure ſcho paſt out of the Toun
To ſeik her Siſter, baith in Dale and Doun.

IV.

THROW mony wilſum Ways then couth ſcho walk,
   Throw Mure and Moſs, throwout Bank, Buſk
      and Breir,
Frae Fur to Fur, cryand frae Balk to Balk,
   Cum furth to me, my awin ſweit Siſter deir,
   Cry, peip anes,—with that the Mous couth heir,
And knew her Voce, as kindly Kinſmen will,
Scho hard with Joy, and furth ſcho came her till.

V.

THAIR hearty Cheir was pleſand to be ſene,
   Quhen thir twa Siſters kind with Blythneſs met,
Quhilk aften Syſs was ſhawin them twa betwein;
   For quhyls they leuch, and quhyls for Joy they grat,
   Quhyls ſweitly kiſt, and quhyls in Arms they plet:
                   And

L

And thus they fure, till ſobirt was thair Meid,
Syne Fute for Fute they to thair Chalmer zeid.

VI.

As I hard ſay, it was a ſemple Wane
  Of Fog and Fern, full feckleſly was maid,
A ſilly Sheil, under a Eard-faſt Stane,
  Of quhilk the Entrie was not hie nor braid;
  Into the ſame they went bot mair abaid,
Withouten Fyre or Candle birnand bricht,
For commonly ſic Pykers luves not Licht.

VII.

Quhen thus wer lugit thir twa ſilly Myce,
  The zungeſt Siſter to her Butrie hyed,
And brocht furth Nuts and Peis inſteid of Spyce,
  And ſic plain Cheir as ſcho had her befyde:
  The Burges Mous ſae dynk and full of Pryde,
Sayd, Siſter myne, Is this zour daylie Fude?
Quhy not, quod ſcho, think ze this Meſs not gude?

VIII.

Na, be my Saul, methink it but a Scorn;
  Madame, quod ſcho, ye be the mair to blame:
My Moder ſaid, aftir that we wer born,

That

That ze and I lay baith within her Wame;
I keip the richt auld Cuſtom of my Dame
And of my Syre,—livand in Povertie,
For Lands and Rents nane is our Propertie.

IX.

My Siſter fair, quod ſcho, haif me excuſt,
  This Dyet rude and I can neir accord;
With tender Meit my Stomock ſtill is uſt,
  For quhy, I fair as weil as ony Lord:
  Thir withert Nuts and Peis, or they be bord,
Will brek my Chafts, and mak my Teith full
    ſklender,
Quhilk has bein uſt before to Meit mair tender.

X.

Weil Siſter, weil then, quoth the rural Mous,
  Gif that ze pleis ſic Things as ze ſe heir,
Baith Meit and Drink, and Herbouray and Hous,
  Sall be zour awin, will ze remain all Zeir,
  Ze ſall it haif with blyth and hairtly Cheir,
And that ſould mak the Meſſes that ar rude,
Still amang Freinds richt tender, ſweit and gude.

XI. Quhat

XI.

QUHAT Pleſans is in Feiſts mair dilicate,
  The quhilk ar given with a gloumand Brow;
A gentle Heart is better recreate
  With Uſage blyth, than ſeith to him a Cow;
  Ane *Modicum* is better, zeill allow,
Sae that Gude-will be Carver at the Deſs,
Than a thrawn Vult, and mony a ſpycie Meſs.

XII.

FOR all this moral Doctrine, ticht and ſoun,
  The Burges Mous had little Will to ſing,
But hevely ſcho keſt her Viſage doun,
  For all the Daintys ſcho couth till her bring;
  Zit at the laſt ſcho ſaid, half in hie thing,
Siſter this Vittell and zour Royal Feiſt
May weil ſuffice for ſic a rural Beiſt.

XIII.

LET be this Hole, and cum unto my Place,
  I ſall zou ſchaw, by gude Experience,
That my *Gude-Frydays* better than zour *Paſe*,
  And a Diſh licking worth zour hale Expence;
  Houſes I haif enow of grit Defence,
Of Cat, nor Fall, nor Trap, I haif nae Dreid:
This ſaid,—that was convinced,—and furth they zeid.

XIV. IN

XIV.

In Skugry ay throw rankeſt Gras and Corn,
  And Wonder flie full prively they creip;
The eldeſt was the Gyde, and went beforn,
  The zunger to her Futeſteps tuke gude keip;
  On Nicht they ran, and on the Day did fleip,
Till on a Morning, or the Lavrock fang,
They fand the Toun, and blythly in couth gang.

XV.

Not far frae thyne, on till a worthy Wane,
  This Burges brocht them fune quhair they fould be,
Without God-fpeid,—thair Herboury was tane
  Intill a Spence, wher Vittell was Plenty,
  Baith Cheis and Butter on lang Skelfs richt hie,
With Fifh and Flefh enough baith frefh and falt,
And Pokks full of Grots, Barlie, Meil and Malt.

XVI.

Quhen afterwart they wer difpofd to dyne,
  Withouten Grace they wufh and went to meit,
On every Difh that Cuikmen can divyne,
  Muttone and Beif cut out in Telzies grit,
  Ane Erles Fair thus can they counterfitt,
Exept ane Thing,—they drank the Watter cleir
Infteid of Wyne, but zit they made gude Cheir.

XVII. With

XVII.

With blyth Upcaſt and merry Countenance,
　　The elder Siſter then ſpeird at her Geſt,
Gif that ſcho thocht be Reſon Differance
　　Betwixt that Chalmer and her ſary Neſt;
　　Zea Dame, quoth ſcho? but how lang will this leſt?
For evermair I wate, and langer to;
Gif that be trew, ze ar at Eiſe, quoth ſcho.

XVIII.

To eik the Cheir, in Plenty furth ſcho brocht
　　A Plate of Grots, and a large Diſh of Meil,
A Threfe of Caiks, I trow ſcho ſpairt them nocht,
　　Abundantlie about her did ſcho deil;
　　Furmage full fyne ſcho brocht inſtead of Geil,
A Candle quhyte out of a Coffer ſtaw,
Inſteid of Spyce, to creiſh thair Teith with a.

XIX.

Thus made they mirry, quhyle they micht nae mair,
　　And hail *Zule!* hail! they all cryt up on hie;
But after Joy ther aftentymes comes Cair,
　　And Trouble after grit Proſperitie:
　　Thus as they ſat in all thair Solitie,
The Spens came on them with Keis in his Hand,
Apent the Dore, and them at Dinner fand.

XX. They

XX.

THEY tarriet not to waſh, ze may ſuppoſe,
　But aff they ran, quha micht the foremoſt win;
The Burges had a Hole, and in ſcho gaes,
　Her Siſter had nae Place to hyde her in,
　To ſee that ſilly Mous it was grit Sin,
Sae diſalait and will of all gude reid,
For very Feir ſcho fell in Swoun, neir deid.

XXI.

BUT as *Jove* wald, it fell a happy Caſe,
　The Spenſar had nae Laiſar lang to byde,
Nowthir to force, to ſeik, nor ſkar, nor cheſe,
　But on he went, and keſt the Dore upwyde;
　This Burges then his Paſage weil has ſpyd,
Out of her Hole ſcho came, and cryt on hie,
How! Siſter fair, cry, peip, quhair eir thou be.

XXII.

THE Landwart Mous lay flatlings on the Ground,
　And for the Deid ſcho was full fair dreidand,
For to her Heart ſtrak mony a waefull Stound,
　As in a Fever trymblit ſcho Fute and Hand;
　And when her Siſter in ſic Plicht her fand,
For very Pitie ſcho began to greit;
Syne Comfort gaif, with Words as Huny ſweit.

XXIII. QUHY

XXIII.

Quhy ly ze thus? Ryfe up my Sifter deir,
  Cum to zour Meit, this Perell is owre-paft;
The uther anfwert, with a hevy Cheir,
  I may nocht eit, fae fair I am agaft:
  I lever had this fourtie lang Days faft,
With Watter Kail, and gnaw dry Beins and Peis,
Then haif zour Feift with this Dreid and Waneife.

XXIV.

With Tretie fair, at laft, fcho gart her ryfe,
  To Burde they went, and down togither fat;
But fkantly had they drunken anes or twyce,
  Quhen in came Hunter *Gib*, the joly Cat,
  And bad God-fpeid.——The Burges up fcho gat,
And till her Hole fcho fled lyk Fyre frae Flint;
But Badrans be the Back the uther hint.

XXV.

Frae Fute to Fute he keft her to and frae,
  Quhyls up, quhyls doun, als tait as ony Kid;
Quhyls wald he let her ryn beneth the Strae,
  Quhyls wald he wink and play with her Buk-hid:
  Thus to the filly Mous grit Harm he did;
Till at the laft, throw fair Fortune and Hap,
Betwixt the Dreffour and the Wall fcho crap.

XXVI. Syne

XXVI.

SYNE up in hafte behind the Pannaling,
  Sae hie fcho clam, that *Gibby* might not get her,
And be the Cluks fae craftylie can hing,
  Till he was gane, her Cheir was all the better.
  Syne down fcho lap, quhen ther was nane to let her.
Then on the Burges Mous alloud did cry,
Sifter fairweil, heir I thy Feift defy.

XXVII.

WER I anes in the Cot that I cam frae,
  For Weil nor Wae I fould neir cum again.
With that fcho tuke her Leif, and furth can gae,
  Quhyles throw the Riggs of Corn, quhyles owre
    the Plain,
  Quhen fcho was furth and frie, her Heart was fain,
And merrylie fcho linkit owre the Mure,
Needlefs to tell how afterwart fcho fure.

XXVIII.

BUT this in fchort fcho reikt her eify Den,
  As warm as on fuppofe it was not grit,
Full beinly ftuffit it was baith butt and ben,
  With Peis, and Nuts, and Beins, and Ry and
    Quheit,
  When eir fcho lykt fcho had eneuch of Meit,

In

In Eife and Quiet, withouten Sturt and Dreid,
But till her Sifter's Feift nae mair fcho zeid.

The MORALITIE.

XXIX.

HEIR ze may find, my Freinds, gif ze tak Heid
    Unto this Fable a gude Moralitie,
As Fitches minglit ar with noble Seid,
    Sae interwoven is Adverfitie
    With eardly Joy, fo that nae State is free,
Withouten Trouble and aft grit Vexation,
    And namelie thay that wreftle up maift hie,
And not contentit ar of fmall Poffefion.

XXX.

BLISSIT be fymple Lyfe, withouten Dreid,
    Bliffit be fober Feift in Quietie;
Quha has eneuch of nae mair has he Neid,
    Thocht it be litle into Quantitie,
    Aboundance grit and blind Profperitie
Maks aftentymes a very ill Conclufion:
    The fweiteft Lyfe therefore in this Countrie
Is Sickernefs and Peace with fmall Poffefion.

XXXI. O

XXXI.

O wanton Man, quhilk ufes ay to feid
  Thy Wame, and maks it maiſt thy God to be,
Luke to thy felf I warn thee weil on Deid;
    For the Cat cums, and to the Mous has Ee,
    Quhat does avail thy Feiſt and Ryelty,
With dreidfull Hairt, and endleſs Tribulation:
    Therefore beſt Thing on Eard, I fay for me,
It is a merry Mynd and ſmall Poſſefion.

XXXII.

FREIND, thy awin Fyre, thocht it be but ane Gleid,
    Will warm thee weil, and is worth Gold to thee;
And *Salamon* the Sage, fays, (gif ze reid,)
    Under the Hevin I can nocht better ſe,
    Than ay be blyth, and leif in Honeſtie.
Quhairfore I may conclude me with this Reafon,
    Of Eardly Blifs it beirs the beſt Degree,
Blythneſs of Hairt in Peace with ſmall Poſſefion.

                    Quod Mr. R. HENRYSON.

ADVICE to his zoung KING.

I.

PRECELAND Prince, haiffing Prerogatyve,
    Of Royal Richt in this Region to ring,
I thee befeik againft thy Luft to ftryve,
    And luve thy GOD aboif all uther Thing,
    And him implore now in thy Zeirs zing
To grant thee Grace thy Subjects to defend,
    Quhilk he has given to thee in governing
In Peice and Honour to thy Lyves End.

II.

AND fen thou ftands in fic a tender Age,
    That Nature zit to thee Wifdome denys;
Therefore fubmit unto thy Council fage,
    And in all Manner work as thay devyfe:
                      But

But ower all Things keip thee frae Covetyfe,
To princely Honour gif thou wald pretend,
 Be liberal ay, then fall thy Fame upryfe,
And win thee Honour to thy Lyves End.

.

III.

GIF that thou gives dilyver quhen thou hechts,
 And nevir let thy Hand thy Hecht delay;
For then thy Hecht and thy Diliverance fechts,
 Far bettir war thy Hecht had biden away;
 He awis me nocht that fchortly fays me nay;
But he that hechts, and caufes me attend,
 Syne gives me not, I may repute him ay,
Ane untrue Dettor to my Lyves End.

IV.

BETTER is the Gut in Feit, than Cramp in Hands,
 The Falt of Feit with Horfe thou may fupport;
But quhen thy Hands are bundin up with Bands,
 Nae Surrigiane may cure them, nor Comfort;
 But thou them open payntit as a Port,
And freily give fic Gudes as GOD dois fend,
 Then may thay mend within a Seafon fchort,
And win the Honour to thy Lyves End.

V. GIVE

V.

GIVE every Man aftir his Faculty,
  And with Difcration ftill difpone thy Geir:
Give not to Fules, and cunning Men ower flie,
  Tho Fules fould roun and flattir in thine Eir,
  Give not to them that dois thy Saws fweir,
Give to them that are true and conftant kend;
  Then ower all quhair thy Fame they fall forth beir,
And win the Honour to thy Lyves laft End.

VI.

SEN thou art Heid, thy Leiges Members all,
  Given by GOD unto thy Governance,
Luke that thou rule the Rute originall,   [vance.
  That throw thy Falt no Limb make other Gri-
  For quha cannot himfelf gyde and advance?
Quhy fould a Provence upon him depend,
  To gyde himfelf that has nae Purveance,
With Peice and Honour to his Lyves laft End?

VII.

DREID GOD, do Council, of thy Leiges leil
  Reward gude Deid, punifh all Wrang and Vyce,
Thoch that thy Saw be ficker as thy Seil,
  Fleme Frawd and be Deffender of Juftice.

                                        Honour

Honour all Time thy noble Genterice,
Obey the Kirk; gif thou dois mifs, amend,
    Sae fall thou win a Place in Paradyce,
And mak on Eard an honourable End.

Quod HEN. STEWART.

ON

CONSCIENS.

I.

QUHEN Doctors preicht to win the Joy eternal,
    Into the Heavens, aftir our LORDS Afcens
They Juftice taught bot Bud or Favour carnal,
    And cauft be punifht flefhly vyl Offens,
Gave Benifice to Clerks of *CONSCIENS;*
    And fae the Feynd had fic Envy thereon.
    Away he gart frae *Confciens* fcrape the *Con,*
And then behind was only left *Sciens.*

II. THEN

II.

THEN were all Clerks for *Sciens* ſune promovit,
 And them that wald to Study maiſt apply:
But zit the Feynd at *Sciens* was comuvit,
 And gart frae *Sciens* ſcrape away the *Sci.*
Sae only *Ens* was left by his ſlie Envy,
 Quhilk ay ſould be for Gold and Geir expont,
 Quhairby Benifices are now diſpont
But *Conſciens* or *Sciens* to ſell and buy.

III.

O Sovraign LORD, and maiſt excellent King,
 Gar put the *Con* and *Sci* again to *Ens,*
And rule thy Realm with Juſtice in thy Ring;
 Give Benifice to Clerks of *Conſciens,*
With Truth and Honour to ſtand thy Defens:
 Sae in thy Court that *Conſciens* be clene,
 For vyle Corruption or thy Days has bene,
Againſt Juſtice, with uthir great Offens.

Quod STEWART.

On the *CREATION, and PARADYCE loſt.*

I.

GOD by His Word His Wark began,
   To form this Erth and Hevin for Man,
      The Sie and Watter deip;
The Sun, the Mune and Stars ſae bricht,
The Day devydit from the Nicht,
      Thair Courſes juſt to keip;
The Beiſts that on the Grund do muve,
      And Fiſhes in the Sie;
Fowls in the Air to flie abuve,
      Of ilk Kind formed HE:
         Sum creiping, ſum fleiting,
         Sum fleing in the Air,
         Sae heichly, ſae lichtly,
         In muving heir and thair.

                              II. THIR

M

II.

THIR Warks of gret Magnificence,
Perfytit by His Providence,
          According to His Will:
Nixt He made Man; To gife him Glore,
Did with His Image him decore,
          Gaife Paradyce him till;
Into that Garden hevinly wrocht,
          With Pleafures mony a one,
The Beifts of every Kynd wer brocht,
          Thair Names he fuld expone;
               Thefe kenning and nameing,
               As them he lift to call,
               For eifing and pleifing
               Of Man, fubdued them all.

III.

IN heavenly Joy Man fae poffeft,
To be alane GOD thocht not beft,
          Made *Eve* to be his Maik;
Bad them increafs and multiplie,
And of the Fruit frae every Tree
          Thair Pleafure they fuld take,

                              Except

Except the Tree of Gude and Ill
    That in the Midſt dois ſtand,
Forbad that they ſuld cum thertill,
     Or twitch it with thair Hand;
      Leſt luking and plucking,
      Baith they and all thair Seid,
      Seveirly, awſteirly,
      Suld die without Remeid.

IV.

Now *Adam* and his luſty *Wyfe*
In Paradyce leidand thair Lyfe,
    With Pleaſures infineit;
Wanting nae thing ſuld do them Eaſe,
The Beiſts obeying them to pleiſe,
    As they could wiſh in Spreit:
Behald the Serpent ſullenlie
    Envyand Mans Eſtate,
With wicket Craft and Subtiltie
    Eve temptit with Deſait;
     Nocht feiring, but ſpeiring,
     Quhy ſcho tuke not her till,
     In uſing and chuſing
     The Fruit of Gude and Ill?

       V. Com-

V.

COMMANDIT us, fcho faid, the LORD,
Noways therto we fuld accord,
  Undir eternall Pain;
But grantit us full Libertie
To eit the Fruit of every Tree,
  Except that Tree in plain.
No, no, nocht fae, the Serpent faid,
  Thou art defaifet therin;
Eit ze therof, ze fall be made
  In Knawledge lyke to Him,
   In feiming and deiming
   Of every thing aricht,
   As dewlie, as trewly,
   As ze wer Gods of Micht.

VI.

EVE thus with thefe fals Words allurit,
Eit of the Fruit, and fyne procurit
  Adam the fame to play:
Behald, faid fcho, how precious,
Sae dilicate and delicious,
  Befyde Knawledge for ay:

Adam

Adam puſt up in warldly Glore,
     Ambition and high Pryd,
Eit of the Fruit; allace therfore,
     And ſae they baith did ſlyd;
        Neglecting, forzetting
        The eternall GODS Command,
        Quha ſcurged and purged
        Them quyt out of that Land.

VII.

QUHEN they had eiten of that Fruit,
Of Joy then war they deſtitute,
     And ſaw thair Bodys bare.
Annon they paſt with all thair Speid,
Of Leives to mak themſelves a Weid,
     To cleith them, was thair Care:
During the Tyme of Innocence,
     Nae Sin or Schame they knew,
Frae Tyme they gat Experience,
     Unto ane Buſs they drew,
        Abyding and hyding,
        As GOD ſuld not them ſee,
        Quha ſpyed, and cryed,
        Adam, *quhy hyds thou thee?*

VIII. I

VIII.

I being naikit, LORD, throu Feir,
For Schame I durſt not to compeir,
  And ſae I did refuſe:
Had thou not eiten of the Tree,
That Knawledge had not bein in thee,
  Nor zit nae ſic Excuſe;
The Helper, LORD, thou gaife to me,
  Has cawſit me to tranſgreſs,
Sayd ſcho, the Serpent ſubtillie,
  Perſuadit me nae leſs,
   Intreiting, be eiting,
   That we ſuld be perfyte,
   Me fylit, begylit;
  In him lyes all the Wyte.

IX.

JEHOVE that evir juged richt,
Bringing His Juſtice to the Licht,
  The Serpent firſt did juge:
Becauſe the Woman thou begylt,
For evir thou ſall be exylt,
  Said He, without Refuge;

       Betwixt

Betwixt her Seid and thy Offfpring
  Nae Peace nor Reft fall be,
And hir Seid fall thy Heid doun thring,
  For all thy Subtiltie;
   Abhorred, deformed,
   Thou on thy Breift fall gang,
   In feiding and leiding
   Thy Lyfe the Beifts amang.

X.

THE Woman nixt, for her Offence,
Did of the LORD refave Sentence,
  Her Sorrow fuld encreafe, .
With Wae and Pain her Childrene beir,
Subdewt to Man, under his Feir,
  No Libertie poffefs:
For *Adams* Falt he curfd the Erth,
  That barrane it fuld be,
Without Labour fuld zield nae Birth
  Of Corns, nor Herb, nor Tree;
   Bot working and irking
   For evir fuld remain,
   And being in deing,
   In Erth returnd again.

XI. O

XI.

O cruel Serpent venemous,
Difpytfull and feditious,
      The Grund of all our Care;
Thou fals-bound Slave unto the Devill,
Thou firft Inventar of this Evill
      Of Blifs, quhilk made us bare;
O devlifh Slave, did thou believe,
      Or hou had thou fic Grace,
Therby for evir thou micht live
      Abuve into that Place:
         Thy Grudging gat Scrudging,
         And fae GOD lute the fe,
        Defavers no Cravers
        Of His Reward fuld be.

XII.

O dainty Dame, with Eirs bent
That harkent to that fals Serpent,
      Thy Bains we may fair ban;
Without Excufe thou art to blame,
Thou juftly has obtaint that Name,
      The very *Wo of Man*:

                      With

With Teirs we may bewail and greit
  That wickit Tyme and Tyde,
Quhen *Adam* was obligit to ſleip,
   And thou tane off his Syde.
    No Sleiping bot Weiping
    Thy Seid hes fund ſenſyne,
    Thy Eiting and Sweiting,
    Is turn'd to Wo and Pyn.

XIII.

ADAM, thy Part, quha can excuſe,
With Knawledge thou that did abuſe
  Thyne awn Felicitie.
The Serpent his inventing fals,
The Womans ſune conſenting als,
  Was nocht ſae wicketly.
GOD did prefer thee to this Day,
  And them ſubdewt to thee,
Sae all that they culd mein or ſay,
  Suld not have moved thee
   To brecking, abjecting
   That hie Command of Lyfe
   Quhilk gydid, provydit
   The ay to live bot Stryf.

      XIV. Be-

XIV.

BEHALD the State that Man was in,
And als how it he tynt throw Sin,
　　And loft the fame for ay;
Zet GOD His Promife dois perform,
Sent His Son of the Virgin born,
　　Our Ranfome deir to pay.
To that great GOD let us give Glore,
　　To us has bein fae gude,
Quha be His Grace did us reftore,
　　Quherof we were denude;
　　　Not careing nor fparing
　　　His Body to be rent,
　　　Redeiming, releiving
　　　Us quhen we wer all fchent.

Quod Sir RICH^{d.} MAITLAND
of *Lethingtoun,* K^{nt.}

The Devils Advice to all and sundry of his best Freinds.

I.

THIS Nicht in Sleip I was agaſt,
Methocht the Deil was tempand faſt,
People with Aiths of Crueltie,
Sayand as throw the Fair he paſt,
Renunce zour GOD, and cum to me.

II.

METHOCHT as he went forth the Way,
A Preiſt ſweirt braid be GOD verry,
Quhilk at the Alter reſſavit he:
Thou art my Clerk, the Deil can ſay,
Renunce thy Creid, and cum to me.

III.

THEN ſwore a Courtier of grit Pryd,
Be Chryſts Woundis bludy and wyd,
And be his Harmis was rent on Tree;
Then ſpak the Deil hard him beſyd,
Renunce thy Creid, and cum to me.

IV. A

IV.

A *Merchant* as he Geir did fell,
Renuncit his Part of Heaven for Hell:
　　The Deil cryd, Welcome mot thou be,
Thou fall be Merchand for my fell,
　　Renunce thy Creid, and cum to me.

V.

A *Goldsmith* faid, This Goldis fae fyne,
That all the Warkmanfhip I tyne,
　　The Feynd reffaife me, gif I lie.
Think on, quod *Nik*, that thou art myne;
　　Renunce thy Creid, and cum to me.

VI.

A *Tailzior* faid, In all this Town,
Be thair a bettir weil made Gown,
　　I gife me to the Feynd all frie:
Gramercy Tailzeor, faid *Mahoun*,
　　Renunce thy Creid, and cum to me.

VII.

A *Soutar* faid, In gude Effeck,
Nor I be hangit be the Neck,
　　Gif better Butes of Lether be.
Fy, quoth the Deil, thou fawrs of Blek,
　　Gae clenge the clene, and cum to me.

VIII. A

VIII.

A *Baxter* ſaid, I quat with God,
And all His Warks baith even and od,
   Gif fyner Stuff ther neids to be.
The Devil leuch, and gae him a Nod,
   Renunce thy Creid, and cum to me.

IX.

The *Fleſhour* ſwore be Sacrament,
And be the Blude maiſt inocent,
   Neir fattir Fleſh Man ſaw with Ee.
The Deil ſaid, Hald on thy Intent,
   Renunce thy Creid, and cum to me.

X.

The *Maltman* ſays, I Bliſs forſake,
And may the Deil of Hell me taik,
   Give ony better Malt may be,
And of this Kill I haif Inlaik,
   Says Sathan, Cum thy Ways to me.

XI.

A *Browſter* ſwore the Malt was ill,
Baith reid and reikit on the Kill,
   It will be nae Ale worth a Flie;
A Boll will not ſax Gallons fill:
   Mahoun cryis, Cum and maſk with me.

XII. The

XII.

THE *Smith* he fwore be Rude and Raip,
Intill a Gallows mot I gaip,
   Gif I ten Days win Pennies three,
For laik of Ale I Water laip:
   Quod *Nic*, Thoull get far les with me.

XIII.

A *Minftrel* faid, The Feynd me ryve,
Gif I do ocht but drink and yve:
   The Deil faid, Hardly mot it be,
Exerce that Craft throu all thy Lyfe,
   And thouill be fure to cum to me.

XIV.

A *Dycer* bad, with Words of Stryf,
The Deil cum ftick him with a Knyf;
   But he keft up fair Syces three:
The Deil faid, Endit is thy Lyfe,
   Renunce thy Creid, and cum to me.

XV.

A *Theif* faid, Ill that eir I chaip,
Nor a ftark Woddy gar me gaip,
   But I in Hell for Geir wald be.
The Deil faid, Welcom in a Raip,
   Gae lift a Cow, and cum to me.

XVI. THE

XVI.

THE Fiſh-wyves flet, and ſwore with Granes,
And to *Auld-nick* ſauld Fleſh and Banes,
   And gaif them with a Schout on hie.
The Deil cryd, Welcome all attaines,
   Sling by zour Creils, and cum to me.

XVII.

METHOCHT the Deils as blak as Pik,
Soliſand were as Beis thick,
   Ay tempand Folk with Ways flie,
Rounand to *Robin* and to *Dick*,
   Renunce zour Creid, and cum to me.

Quod DUNBAR.

THE

THE

Claith-Merchant;

Or, a Ballat made on Jonet Reid, Jean
Violet, *and* Anna Whyt, *being flicht*
Women, and Taverners.

I.

O F Collours cleir,
  Quha lykes to weir,
Are mony Sorts into this Toun,
  Grene, Zellow, Blew,
  And ilka Hew,
Baith *Paris* Black, and *Inglis* Broun;
  Braw *London* Sky,
  Quha lykes to buy,
Colour de Roy is clene laid down,
  And *Dunde* Gray
  This mony a Day
Is lichtlyt baith be Lad and Loun.

II. But

II.

But ftanch my Fyking,
And ftryd my Lyking,
Are feimly Hews for Simmer Play;
Din dipt in Zellow
For ilka gude fallow,
As *Will* of *Quhyt-hauch* bad me fay;
I will not deny it
To them that will buy it,
For Silver nane fall be faid nay;
Ze neid not plenze,
It will not ftenzie,
Suppofe ye weit it Nicht and Day.

III.

And I have *Quhyt*
Of great Delyt,
And *Violet* quha lykes to weir,
Weil wearand *Reid*
Till ze be dead;
It fall not failzie, tak ze no Feir.
The *Quhyt* is gude,
And richt weil lued,

But

N

But zit the *Reid* is twice as deir:
    The *Violet* fyne,
    Baith frefh and fyne,
Sall ferve ye Hofeing for a Zeir.

IV.

THE *Quhyt* is teuch,
    And frefh enouch,
Saft as the Silk, as all Men feis.
    The *Reid* is bonny,
    And focht be mony;
They hyve about the Houfe lyke Beis.
    My *Violet* faft,
    Quhen ye have coft,
Will ply lyk Satin to zour Theis;
    Sure be my witting
    Not burnt in the Litting,
Suppofe baith Lads and Limmers leis.

V.

OF thir thrie Hews
    I haif left Clews,
To be our Court-Men Winter Weid,

Weill

Weill twynt and fmal,
The beft of them all
May weir the Claith for Woul and Threid;
But in the Wawk-mill,
The Wedder is ill:
Thefe are not drying Days indeid;
And gif it be wat,
I hecht for that,
It tuggs in Holes and gaes abreid.

VI.

Zit its weil wawkit,
Cardit and cawkit,
As warm a Weid as weir the Dule,
Weil wrocht in Luims,
With Wobfters Guims,
Baith thick and nymble gaes the Spule;
Cottond and fhorn,
The mair it be worn,
Ze will find zour fell the greater Fule,
Zit bony forfuith,
Cum buyit in my Buith,
To mak ze Garments againft Zule.

VII. Thir

VII.

Thir mixt togither,
Zour fell may confider,
Quhat fyner Colour can there be fund,
And namely for Breiks,
Gif ony Man feiks,
Heill purchace the Pair ay for a Pund:
Abeit it be fkant,
Nae Wowars fall want,
That to my bidding will be bund,
Weil may they bruik it,
They neid not luke it,
But grape it Mirklyns be the Grund.

VIII.

Our Court-Men heir,
Has made my Claith deir,
Raifd it Twall-penies of ilka Ell,
Zit is my Claith fure,
Beft Sadles to cure,
Suppofe the hale Seffion fhould ryd themfel.
The *Violet* certain,
Was maid at *Dumbartain;*
The *Reid* was wawkit at *Dunkell:*

The

The *Quhyt* has bein dicht
In mony mirk Nicht,
But Tyme and Place I cannot weil tell.

IX.

Now gif ye work wyflie,
And fhape it precyflie;
The Ellwand   *   *   *
Gif the Bys be wyde,
Gar lay it on Syde;
And fae ze cannot weil gae wrang;
And for the lang Lift,
It wald be fewd faft,
And care not by how deip ze gang;
But want ze quhyt Threid,
Ye will not cum fpeid,
Black Waluway maun be zour Sang.

X.

And tho it be auld,
And Twenty Tymes fald,
Zit will the Freprie ot mak ze fain,

With

With Oyls to renew it,
And mak it weil hewt,
And gar it glans lyk Silk in Grain;
Syne with the fleik Stains
That feryis for the Nains,
They raife the Pyle quhen it falls plain:
With mony braid Aith,
We fell this fame Claith,
To gar the Buyers cum faft again.

XI.

Now is my Wob wrocht,
And arlet and bocht,
Cum lay the Payment in my Hand;
And gif my Claith felzie,
Zeis not pay a Melzie,
The Wob fall be at zour Command.
The Market is thrang,
And will not laft lang;
They buy faft in the Border Land;
Abeit I haif Tinfel;
Zit maun I tak Handfell,
To pay my Buith-Mail and my Stand.

XII. My

XII.

My Claith wald be lude,
Be great Men of gude,
Gif Lads and Lowns wald let me be,
Zit maun I excuſe them;
How can I refuſe them,
Sen all Mens Penny maks him frie?
The beſt and Gay ot,
My ſelf tuke a Sey ot,
A Wylie-coat I will nocht lie,
Quhilk did me nae Harm,
But held my Coſt warm,
A ſymple Merchant ye may ſee.

XIII.

This far to relive me,
That nane may reprive me,
In *Jedbrugh* at the Juſticeair,
This Sang of thrie Laſſes
Was made abune Glaſſes,
That Tyme that they wer Tapſters thair.
The firſt was a *Quhyt*,
A Laſs of Delyte;

The

The *Violet* was baith gude and fair:
  Keip *Reid* frae all Skaith.
  Scho is wordie them baith;
Sae to be ſhort I ſay nae mair.

Quod SEMPLE.

On King JAMES V. *his three Miſtreſſes.*

SAw not thy Seid on *Sandylands*,
  Spend not thy Strength on *Weir*,
And ryd not on the *Oliphant*,
  For hurting of thy Geir.

THE

THE

LYON and the MOUS.

I.

IN Midſt of *June*, that jolly Seaſon ſweit,
    Quhen *Phebus* fair, with his warm Beams ſae
      bricht
Had dryit frae Dale and Dawn the dewy Weit,
    And all the Land made with his leiming Licht,
    In a gay Morn, betwixt Mid-day and Nicht,
I raiſe and put all Slouth and Sleip on Syde,
And went allone untill a Forreſt wyde.

II.

SWEIT was the Smell of Flowirs, blae, quhyt and
      reid,
    The Noyſe of Birds was maiſt melodious,
The bobing Bews bluimd braid abune my Heid,
    The Grund growand with Graſs maiſt verderous,
    Of all Pleiſance that Place was plenteous,
With ſweit Odour and Birds ſaft Hermonie,
The Morning myld increaſd the Mirth and Glee.

III. THE

III.

The Rofes reid arrayt the Rone and Ryfs,
  The Primrofe and the Purpure Violae;
To heir it was a Poynt of Paradyce,
  Sic Mirth the Mavis and the Merle couth mae;
  The Blofoms blyth brak up on Bank and Brae,
The Smell of Herbs, and the Wing-minftrell Cry,
Contending quha fould haif the Victory.

IV.

Me to conferve frae the Suns birning Heit,
  Undir the Schadow of an Awthorn-grene,
I leant me doun amang the Flowirs fweit,
  Syn made a Crofs, and closed baith myne Een;
  On Sleip I fell amang the Bewis bein,
And in my Dream methocht came throw the Schaw
The faireft Man that eir before I faw.

V.

His Goun was of a Claith as quhyte as Milk,
  His Chymers wer of Chamelet Purpure broun,
His Hude of Scarlet, borderit round with Silk
  In hekle Ways, untill his Girdle doun;
  Of the auld Faffoun was his Bonnat roun,
His Heid was quhyt, his Een was grene and gray,
With lokar Hair, quhilk owre his Shulder lay.

VI. A

VI.

A Row of Paper in his Hand he bair,
  A Swans quhyt Pen ſtickand beneth his Eir,
Ane Inkhorn with a pretty gilt Pennair,
  A Bag of Silk, all at his Belt he weir;
  Thus was he gudely grathit in his Geir,
Of Stature large, and with a feirfull Face,
To quher I lay he came with ſturdy Pace.

VII.

AND ſayd, God-ſpeid, my Son, and I was fain
  Of that couth Word, and of his Company;
With Reverence I ſalutet him again,
  Welcome Fader, and he ſat doun by me;
  Diſpleis zou not, my gude Maſter, tho I
Demand zour Birth, zour Facultie and Name,
Quhat brings ze hier, and quher ze dwell at hame?

VIII.

MY Son, he ſayd, I am of gentle Blude,
  My natall Land is *Rome*, withouten nay,
And in that Toun firſt to the Schulis I zied,
  And ſtudyt Sciens ther full mony a Day,
  And now my winning is in Heaven for ay;
Eſope I hecht my Wryting and my Wark,
Is couth and kend to many a cunnand Clark.

IX. O

IX.

O Maifter *Efope*, Poet and Laureat,
    God wate ze are full deir welcome to me;
Are ze not he that all thir Fables wrat,
    Quhilk in Effect, altho they fenziet be,
    Are full of Prudence and Moralitie?
Fair Son, he fayd, I am the famyne Man;
My flichterand Heart I wate grew mirry than.

X.

ESOPE, faid I, my Maifter venerable,
    I heartilie zou befeik, for Cheritie,
Ze wald dedene to tell a pritty Fable,
    Concludand with a gude Moralitie;
    Schekand his Heid, he fayd, My Son let be,
For quhat ift worth to tell a fenziet Tale,
Quhen hale preiching may naithing now avail?

XI.

Now in this Warld methinks richt few or nane
    To haly Scripture has the leift Regaird;
The Eir is deif, the Hairt is hard as Stane,
    They nevir mynd Punition or Rewaird,
    Thair Lukes inclynand allways to the Eard;
Sae rouftet is the Warld with Canker black,
That all my Tales may little Succour mak.

XII. Zit

XII.

Zit gentle Sr, fayd I, for my Requieſt,
  Not to diſpleis zour Fatherheid I pray,
Undir the Figure of ſum brutal Beiſt,
  A moral Fable ze wald grant to ſay;
  Quha kens nor I may leir and beir away
Sumthing therby, hereaftir may avail:
I grant, quoth he, and thus began his Tale.

XIII.

A Lyon at his Prey weiry forrun,
  To recreate his Limbs and tak his Reſt,
Beikand his Breiſt and Bellie at the Sun,
  Undir a Tree lay in the fair Foreſt;
  Then came a Trip of Myce out of thair Neſt,
Richt tait and trig, all danſand in a Gyſs,
And owre the Lyon lanſit twyſs or thryſs.

XIV.

He lay ſae ſtill, the Myce was not affeird,
  But to and frae atowre him tuke thair Trace;
Sum tirlt at the Whiskers of his Beird,
  Sum did not ſpare to claw him on the Face:
  Merry and glade thus danſit they a Space,
Till at the laſt the nobil Lyon wouk,
And with his Paw the Maiſter Mous he tuke.

XV. He

XV.

HE gaif a Cry, and all the laif agaſt,
  Their Danſing left, and hid them heir and thair;
He that was tane cryit out and weipit faſt,
  And ſayd, Allace for now and evermair!
  Now am I tane a wofull Priſoner,
And for my Gilt believes incontinent
Jugement to thole, and unto Death be ſent.

XVI.

THEN ſpak the Lyon to that carefull Mous,
  Thou catyve Wretch, and vyle unwordy Thing,
Owre malapert and owre preſumpteous,
  Thou was to mak atowre me thy Tripping;
  Know thou not weil I was baith Lord and King
Of all the Beiſts?—This (quod the Mous) I knaw,
But I miſknew, becauſe ze lay ſae law.

XVII.

LORD, I beſiek thy Princely Ryaltie,
  Heir quhat I ſay, and tak in Patience;
Conſidder firſt my ſimple Povertie,
  And ſyne thy mighty high Magnificence;
  Se als how Things that is done by negligence,
Not frae malicious Thocht, or ill deſynd,
Sould gain Remiſſion frae a Kingly Mynd.

                    XVIII. WITH

XVIII.

WITH gret Aboundance we wer all repliet
  Of alkynd Fude, fic as to us affeird,
And us to dans, provokit the Seafon fweit,
  And mak fic Mirth as Nature to us laird;
  Ze lay fae ftill and law upon the Eard,
That be my Saul we weind ze had bein deid,
Ells wald we not haif danfit owre zour Heid.

XIX.

THY falfe Excufe, the Lyon fayd again,
  Sall not avail a Myt, I undertae;
I put the Cafe, had I bene deid or flain,
  And fyne my Skin bene ftapit full of Strae,
  Thocht thou had found my Figure lyand fae,
Becaufe it bare the Prent of my Perfoun,
Thou fould for Dreid on Kneis haif falen doun.

XX.

Now for thy Cryme thou can mak nae Defence,
  My Ryal Perfon thus to vylipend,
Nowther by Forfs nor thyne oun Negligence,
  For till Excufe thou can nae Caufe prettend;
  Therfore thou fuffer fall a fchamefull End,
And Deid, fic as to Treffon is decreit,
To be hung on a Gallows be the Fiet.

XXI. O

XXI.

O Mercy, Lord! at thy Gentrice I afs,
  As thou art King of all Beifts corronat,
Sobir thy Wrath, and let thyn Yre owrepafs,
  And mak thy Mynd to Mercy inclynat;
  I grant Offens is done to thy Eftate,
Therfore I wirdy am to fuffir Deid,
But gif thy Kingly Mercy reik Remeid.

XXII.

In evry Juge Mercy and Rewth fuld be,
  As Affeffors and collaterall;
Without Mercy, Juftice is Crewelltie,
  As faid is in the Law fpirituall:
  When Rigour fits upon the hygh Tribunall,
The Equitie of Law quha may fuftain?
Richt few or nane bot Mercy gae betwein.

XXIII.

Besyds ze knaw the Honour Triumphs zeild,
  To every Victor, on the Strength depends
Of his Compeir, quhilk manly in the Feild,
  Throw Jepordy of Arms he lang deffends;
  Quhat Pryce or Lowding, quhen the Battle ends,
Is fayd of him that overcomes a Man;
Him to deffend that nowther dow nor can.

XXIV. A

XXIV.

A Thoufand Myce to murder and devore,
   Is litle Manheid in a Lyon ftrang;
Full litle Worfhip can ze win thairfore,
    To quhofe vaft Strenth is nae Comparefon:
    It will degrad fum Part of zour Renown
To flay a Mous that can mak nae Deffence,
But afkand Mercy at zour Excellence.

XXV.

ALso it not becomes zour Celfitude,
   That ufes daylie Meit delicious,
To fyle zour Lipps or Grinders with my Blude,
    Quhilk to zour Stomak is contagious;
    Unhalefom Melteth is a fairy Mous,
And namely to a nobil Lyon ftrang,
Wont to be fed with gentil Venifon.

XXVI.

My Lyfe is litle, and my Deid far lefs;
   Zit, gif I live, I may peraventure
Supplie zour Highnes being in Diftrefs:
    For aft is fene a Man of fmall Stature
    Refkewed has a Lord of hygh Honnour,
Kept that has bene in Poynt to be owre-thrawn,
Throu Fortunes• Falt; fic Cafe me be zour awn.

XXVII. QUHEN

o

XXVII.

Quhen this was fayd, the generous Lyon paufit,
  And thocht this arguing did not Reafon want;
His Yre affwageit, and his kynd Mercy caufit
  Him to the Mous a full Remiffion grant,
  Opent his Paw; He on his Kneis doun bent,
And baith his Hands unto the Heaven upheild,
Cryand, Almichty *Jove* give zou lang Eild.

XXVIII.

Quhen he was gane, the Lyon zeid to hunt,
  For he had nocht, but livd upon his Prey,
And flew baith tame and wyld, as he was wont,
  And in the Countrie made a grit Deray;
  Till at the laft the People fand the Way
This crewell Lyon with a Girn to tak,
Of hempin Cords richt ftrang Netts coud they mak.

XXIX.

And in a Road quhair he was wont to rin,
  With Raips rude frae Trie to Trie it band,
Syne cufte a Raing on Raw the Wod within,
  With Blafts of Horns and Cauits faft calland;
  The Lyon fled, and throu the Rone rinnand
Fell in the Net, and hankit Fute and Heid,
For all his Strenth he coud mak nae Remeid.

XXX. Roland

XXX.

ROLAND about with hydious Rowmiffing,
  Quhyles to quhyles frae, gif he micht Succor get;
But all in vain, that velziet him naething,
  The mair he flang, the fafter he was knit:
  The Raips rude about him fae was plet
On every Syde, that Succor faw he nane,
But ftill lyand, thus murnand maid his Mane.

XXXI.

O fair lameit Lyon, liggand heir fae law,
  Quhair is the Micht of thy Magnificence,
Of quhom all brutal Beift in Eard ftand Aw,
  And dreid to luke on thy gret Excellence;
  Bot Hope or Help, bot Succor or Defence,
In ftrang Hemp-bands heir maun I ly, allace!
Till I be flain, I fe nae uther Grace.

XXXII.

THER is nae Joy that will my Harms wraik,
  Nor Creature to do Comfort to my Crown,
Quha fall me bute? Quha fall thir Bands brek?
  Quha fall me put frae Pain of this Prifon?
  Be that he had his Lamentation done,
Perchance the litle pardond Mous came neir,
And of the Lyon hard the pityous Beir.

XXXIII. AND

XXXIII.

AND fuddainly it came intill his Mynd
 That it fuld be the Lyon did him Grace,
And fayd, Now wer I fals and richt unkynd,
 Bot gif I quit fum Part thy Gentilnefs
 Thou did to me, —— and on with that he gaes
To all his Maiks, and on them faft did cry,
Cum help, cum help; and they came all on hy.

XXXIV.

Lo, quoth the Mous, this is our Ryal Lord,
 Quha gaif me Grace quhen I was by him tane,
And now is faft heir fanklet in a Cord,
 Wrekand his Hurt with Murning fair and Mane,
 Bot we him help, of Suplie kens he nane;
Cum help to quyt ane gude Turn with annither,
Sae beit, cryd all; fyn fell to Wark togither.

XXXV.

THEY tuke nae Knyf, thair Teith wer fherp enewgh;
 To fe that Sicht forfuith it was grit Wonder,
How that they ran amang the Halters tewgh,
 Before, behind, fum zeid abune, fum under,
 And fchure the Raips with the maift eifs in Sunder,
Syne bad him ryfe, —— and he ftart up annone,
And thankit them; fyn to the Bent is gane.
       XXXVI. Now

XXXVI.

Now dois the Lyon frie of Danger fkour,
  Lowfe, and delivert till his Libertie,
By litle Animals of fmalleft Power,
    As ze haif hard, becaufe he had Pitie:
    Quoth I, Maifter, is ther Moralitie
Into this Fable? —— *Son*, fayd he, *richt gude;*
I pray zou gieft, quoth I, or ze conclude.

The MORALITIE.
XXXVII.

WE may fuppofe this Lyon of Renoun
    May fignifie ane Emperour or King,
Or ony Poteftate that weirs a Croun,
    That fould be wakryfe in his governing,
    But of his Peple taks flicht noticeing,
To rule and fteir the Land, and Juftice keip,
But lazy lyes in luftie Slouth and Sleip.

XXXVIII.

THE Foreft fair with Bloffoms lown and lie,
    The fingand Birds and Flowirs fae ferly fweit,
Ar but this Warld, and his Profperitie,
    As Pleifands fals mingillit with Care repleit,
    Richt, as the Rofe with Froft and Winter weit,
Wallous; fae dois the Warld and them defaif
That Confidence in lufty Pleafures haif.

XXXIX. THIR

XXXIX.

THIR litle Myce ar Comonalitie,
　　Wanton, unwyfe, without Corection due;
Sic Lords and Princes, quhen they chanfs to fe
　　That execute, the richteous Laws on few,
　　They dreid naithing, but with rebellious Brow
Dar difobey; for quhy? they ftand nae Aw,
That maks them aft thair Soverains to mifknaw.

XL.

AND be this Fable, Lords of prudent Sence
　　Confidder may the Virtue of Pitie,
And fuld remit fumtyme a grit Offence,
　　And Mercy metigate with Crueltie;
　　Aftymes is fene a Man of fmall Degree
Has quit a Common baith for Gude and Ill,
As Lords has Rigour done, or Grace him till.

XLI.

QUHA wates how fune a Lord of grit Renoun,
　　Rowand in warldly Luft and vain Pleifance,
May be owrthrawin, diftroyed, or put doun
　　Throu Fortune fals, that of all Variance
　　Is hale Miftres, and Leader of the Dance
To lufty Men, and binds them up fae foir,
That they nae Perell can provyd befor.

XLII. THIR

XLII.

THIR crewell Men that ftentit has the Net
  In quhilk the Lyon fuddenlie was tane,
Waited allway that they a Mends micht get;
  For Hurt, Men wryts with Steil in Marble-ftane,
  Mair till expone, as now, I let alane:
But King and Lord may weil wate what I mein,
The Figure hereof aftymes has bein fene.

XLIII.

QUHEN this was fayd, quoth *Efop*, My fair Chyld,
  Perfuade the Kirkmen eydentlie to pray,
That Treafon off this Countrie be exyld,
  That Juftice ring, and Nobles keip their Fay
  Unto thair Soverain Lord baith Nicht and Day:
And with that Word he vaneift, and I woke,
Syne throu the Schaw my Jurney hamewart tuke.

                  Quod Mr. RO. HENRYSON.

THE

THE

TOD and the LAMB,

OR,

Follows the Wowing of the King when he was at Dumfermeling.

I.

THis hinder Nicht in *Dumfermeling*,
 To me was tald a wonder Thing,
That late a Tod was with a Lamb,
And with hir playd, and made gude Game;
 Syne to his Breiſt did hir imbrace,
And wald haif ridden hir lyk a Ram,
 And that methocht a ferly Caſe.

II.

HE braiſt hir bonny Bodie ſweit,
And halſt hir with his forder Feit,
Syne ſchuke his Tail with Whindge and Zelp;
And todlit with hir lyke a Quhelp,
 Then lourit on growf, and aſked Grace;
And ay the Lamb cryd, Lady help,
 And that methocht a ferly Caſe.

III. THE

III.

THE Tod was nowthir lein nor fcowry,
He was a lufty reid-haird *Lowry*,
Ane lang taild Beift and grit withall;
The filly Lamb was all to fmall,
    With fic a Trible to hald a Bafe:
Scho fled him not, fair mot her fall,
    And that methocht a ferly Cafe.

IV.

THE Tod was reid, the Lamb was quhyte,
Scho was a Morfell of Delyte;
He luvit nae Ews auld teuch and Sklender,
Becaufe this Lamb was zung and tender.
    He ran upon her with a Race,
And fcho fchup nevir to defend hir,
    And this methocht a ferly Cafe.

V.

HE gripit her about the Waift,
And handilt her as gif in Hafte;
This Inocent that neir trefpaft,
Tuke Heart that fcho was handilt faft,
    And lute him kifs her lufty Face:
His girnand Gams hir nocht agaft,
    And that methocht a ferly Cafe.

VI. HE

VI.

He held hir till him be the Hals,
And fpake full fair thocht he was fals;
Syne faid and fwore to hir in Mode,
That he fuld not twitch hir Prein-cod.
　The filly Thing trow'd him, allace!
The Lamb gaif Creddance to the Tod,
　And that methocht a ferly Cafe.

VII.

I will nae Leifings put in Verfe,
Lyke as fum Janglers do reherfe;
But be quhat Manner they wer mard,
Quhen Licht was out and Dores were bard:
　I wate not gif he gaif hir Grace;
But Winnocks all were ftappit hard,
　And that methocht a ferly Cafe.

VIII.

Quhen Folk do fleit in Joy maift far,
Thair fune cums Wae or they be War,
Quhen carpand wer thir twa maift croufe,
The Wolf he umbefet the Houfe,
　Upon the Tod to make a Chace:
The Lamb fcho cheipit lyke a Moufe,
　And that methocht a ferly Cafe.

IX. THROW

IX.

THROW hydious Howling of the Wowf,
This wylie Tod plait doun on Growf;
And in the filly wie Lambs Skin,
He crap as far as he micht win,
 And hid him thair a gay lang Space;
The Ews befyde they made nae Din,
 And that methocht a ferly Cafe.

X.

QUHEN of the Tod was heerd nae Peip,
The Wowf wont all had bene afleip;
And quhyle the Tod had ftriken Ten,
The Wowf he dreft him to his Den,
 Proteftand for the fecond Place:
And this Report I with my Pen,
 How at *Dumfermling* fell the Cafe.

Quod DUNBAR.

On

On anes being his own Enemy.

I.

HE that has Gold and Riches great,
    And may live at a merry Rate;
And Gladneſs dois frae him expell,
And lives into a wretched State;
    He worketh Sorrow to himſell.

II.

HE that may be bot Sturt and Stryf,
And live a luſty lightſome Lyfe,
    And ſyne with Marriage dois him mell,
And buckles with a wicked Wyfe,
    He worketh Sorrow to himſell.

III.

HE that has for his awin Genzie
A pleſand Prop bot Mank or Menzie,
    And ſhutes ſyne at an uncow Schell,
And is forfairn with Fleis of *Spenzie*,
    He worketh Sorrow to himſell.

IV. AND

IV.

AND he that with gude Life and Treuth,
Bot Variance or other Slewth,
  Dois evir with a Mafter dwell,
That nevir of him will have Rewth,
  He worketh Sorrow to himfell.

V.

Now all this Time let us be merry,
And fet not by this Warld a Cherry,
  Now quhyle thair is gude Wyne to fell;
The Cheil that dois on dry Breid wirry,
  I give them to the Devil of Hell.

Quod DUNBAR.

*The Benifite of them who have Ladies
wha can be gude Soliciters at Court.*

I.

THIR Ladys fair, that mak Repair,
    And at the Court are kend,
In three Days thair, they will do mair,
    Ane Matter for till end,
Than ther Gude-men will do in Ten,
    For any Craft they can,
Sae weil they ken, what Time and quhen,
    Thair Manes they fuld mak than.

II.

WITH little Noy they can convoy
    A Matter finally,
Richt myld and Moy, and keip it coy,
    On Evens fae quietly;
They do no mifs, but gif they kifs,
    And keip Colation,
Quhat Reck of this, thair Matter is
    Brocht to Conclufion.

III. THEN

III.

THEN wit ye weil, they haif grit Feil,
  And Matter to folift,
Treft as the Steil, fyne neir a Deil,
  Quhen they come hame are mift.
Thir Lairds they are, methink richt far,
  Sic Wyves behalden to,
That fae weil dar gae to the Bar,
  Quhen there is ocht to do.

IV.

THEREFORE I reid, gif ze haif Pleid,
  Or Matter in the Play,
To mak Remeid, fend in zour Steid
  Zour Ladys graitht up gay;
They can deffend, even to the End,
  And Matters forth exprefs;
Suppofe they fpend, it is unkend;
  Thair Geir is nocht the lefs.

V.

IN quiet Place, gin they have Space,
  Within lefs than twa Hours,
They can percafe, purchafe fum Grace,
  At the Compofitours;

Thair

Thair Compofition with full Remiſſioṅ,
   Thair finally is endit,
With Expedition, and full Condition,
   Thair Seals then are to pendit.

VI.

ALL hale almoſt they make the Coſt,
   With ſober Recompence,
Richt little loſt, they get indorſt,
   All hale thair Evidence,
Sic Ladys wyſe, they are to pryze,
   To ſay the Verity,
Sae can devyſe, and not ſurpryze
   Thame nor thair Honeſty.

Quod DUNBAR.

Annother

Annother of the famen Caft,
Pend be the Poet wrote the laft.

I.

THE Ufe of Court richt weil I knaw,
 Ladyis Soliceters of the Law;
  At hame remain the filly Lairds,
  And fend thair Wyves behind the Yards,
  Well ftuft with Money and Rewards,
To furder thair Errands frae Nicht faw.

II.

In Clouks they cum full braw quhyte cled,
And rouns to have thair Matter fped;
  They give nae Budds,
  But on thair Fudds
  They get grit Skuds,
  In nakit Bed.

       III. But

P

III.

BUT neirthelefs the Laird maun fyn,
For all hir Miens, a Tun of Wyne:
  His Wyfe cums hame thus fynely ufd,
  But zit he maun hald hir excufd;
  And finaly the Folks that doift
Denys and laughs at them baith fyne.

IV.

THE Laird murns quhen he may not mend it,
His Lady jaipt his Siller fpend it,
  And all his Labour turnd in vain;
  But ay the Lady fays full plain,
  That fcho maun to the Court again,
Or els the Plea will not be endit.

V.

HIR Buckler bord, and backward born,
And all hir Caufe is quite forlorn;
  Up gets hir Wame,
  Scho thinks nae Schame
  Syne to bring hame
   The Laird a Horn.

THE

THE
VISION.

Compylit in Latin *be a moſt lernit Clerk**
in Tyme of our Hairſhip and Oppreſſion,
anno 1300, *and tranſlatit in* 1524.

I.

BEDOUN the Bents of *Banquo* Brae
   Milane I wandert waif and wae,
     Muſand our main Miſchaunce;
How be thay Faes we ar undone,
That ſtaw the *ſacred*† *Stane* frae *Scone*,
     And leids us ſic a Daunce:

                 Quhyle

---

* The Hiſtory of the *Scots* Sufferings, by the unworthy Con-
deſcenſion of *Baliol* to *Edward* I. of *England,* till they recovered
their Independence by the Conduct and Valour of the Great BRUCE,
is ſo univerſally known, that any Argument to this antique Poem
ſeems uſeleſs.

† The old Chair (now in *Weſtminſter* Abbey) in which the *Scots*
Kings were always crown'd, wherein there is a Piece of Marble with
this Inſcription;

    Ni fallat fatum, SCOTI, *quocunque locatum*
    Invenient lapidem, regnare tenentur ibidem.

Quhyle *Inglands Edert* taks our Tours,
 And *Scotland* ferft obeys,
Rude Ruffians ranfakk Ryal Bours,
 And *Baliol* Homage pays;
  Throch Feidom our Freidom
  Is blotit with this Skore,
  Quhat *Romans* or no Mans
  Pith culd eir do befoir.

II.

THE Air grew ruch with boufteous Thuds,
Bauld *Boreas* branglit outthrow the Cluds,
 Maift lyke a drunken Wicht;
The Thunder crakt, and Flauchts did rift
Frae the blak Viffart of the Lift:
 The Forreft fchuke with Fricht;
Nae Birds abune thair Wing extenn,
 They ducht not byde the Blaft,
Ilk Beift bedeen bangd to thair Den,
 Untill the Storm was paft:
  Ilk Creature in Nature
  That had a Spunk of Sence,
  In Neid then, with Speid then,
  Methocht cryt, In Defence.

III. To

III.

To fe a Morn in *May* fae ill,
I deimt Dame Nature was gane will,
    To rair with rackles Reil;
Quhairfor to put me out of Pain,
And fkonce my Skap and Shanks frae Rain,
    I bure me to a Beil,
Up ane hich Craig that lundgit alaft,
    Out owre a canny Cave,
A curious Cruif of Natures Craft,
    Quhilk to me Schelter gaif;
      Ther vexit, perplexit,
      I leint me doun to weip,
      In brief ther, with Grief ther
      I dottard owre on Sleip.

IV.

HEIR *Somnus* in his filent Hand
Held all my Sences at Command,
    Quhyle I forzet my Cair;
The myldeft Meid of mortall Wichts
Quha pafs in Peace the private Nichts,
    That wauking finds it rare;

Sae

Sae in faft Slumbers did I ly,
But not my wakryfe Mynd,
Quhilk ftill ftude Watch, and couth efpy
A Man with Afpeck kynd,
Richt auld lyke and bauld lyke,
With Baird thre Quarters fkant,
Sae braif lyke and graif lyke,
He feemt to be a Sanct.

V.

GRIT Darring dartit frae his Ee,
A Braid-fword fchogled at his Thie,
On his left Arm a Targe;
A fhynand Speir filld his richt Hand,
Of ftalwart Mak, in Bane and Brawnd,
Of juft Proportions, large;
A various Rain-bow colourt Plaid
Owre his left Spaul he threw,
Doun his braid Back, frae his quhyt Heid,
The Silver Wymplers grew;
Amaifit, I gaifit
To fe, led at Command,
A ftrampant and rampant
Ferfs Lyon in his Hand.

VI. QUHILK

VI.

QUHILK held a Thiftle in his Paw,
And round his Collar graift I faw
    This Poefie pat and plain,
Nemo me impune lacefs-
-Et:—— In Scots, Nane fall opprefs
    Me, unpunift with Pain;
Still fchaking, I durft naithing fay,
    Till he with kynd Accent
Sayd, Fere let nocht thy Hairt affray,
    I cum to hier thy Plaint;
        Thy graining and maining
        Haith laitlie reikd myne Eir,
        Debar then affar then
        All Eirynefs or Feir.

VII.

FOR I am ane of a hie Station,
The *Warden* of this auntient Nation,
    And can nocht do the Wrang;
I viffyt him then round about,
Syne with a Refolution ftout,
    Speird, Quhair he had bene fae lang?

                Quod

Quod he, Althocht I fum forfuke,
    Becaus they did me flicht,
To Hills and Glens I me betuke,
    To them that luves my Richt;
        Quhafe Mynds zet inclynds zet
        To damm the rappid Spate,
        Devyfing and pryfing
        Freidom at ony Rate.

VIII.

OUR Trechour Peirs thair Tyranns treit,
Quha jyb them, and thair Subftance eit,
    And on thair Honour ftramp;
They, pure degenerate! bend thair Baks,
The Victor, *Langfhanks*, proudly cracks
    He has blawn out our Lamp:
Quhyle trew Men, fair complainand, tell,
    With Sobs, thair filent Greif,
How *Baliol* thair Richts did fell,
    With fmall Howp of Releife;
        Regretand and fretand
        Ay at his curfit Plot,
        Quha rammed and crammed
        That Bargin doun thair Throt.

IX. BRAIF

IX.

BRAIF Gentrie fweir, and Burgers ban,
Revenge is muttert be ilk Clan
  Thats to thair Nation trew;
The Cloyfters cum to cun the Evil,
Mailpayers wifs it to the Devil,
  With its contryving Crew:
The Hardy wald with hairty Wills,
  Upon dyre Vengance fall;
The fecklefs fret owre Heuchs and Hills,
  And Eccho Anfwers all,
   Repetand and greitand,
   With mony a fair Alace,
   For Blafting and Cafting
   Our Honour in Difgrace.

X.

WAES me! quod I, our Cafe is bad,
And mony of us are gane mad,
  Sen this difgraceful Paction.
We are felld and herryt now by Forfe;
And hardly Help fort, thats zit warfe,
  We are fae forfairn with Faction.

        Then

Then has not he gude Caufe to grumble,
Thats forft to be a Slaif;
Oppreffion dois the Judgment Jumble
And gars a wyfe Man raif.
May Cheins then, and Pains then
Infernal be thair Hyre
Quha dang us, and flang us
Into this ugfum Myre.

XI.

THEN he with bauld forbidding Luke,
And ftaitly Air did me rebuke,
For being of Sprite fae mein:
Said he its far beneath a *SCOT*
To ufe weak Curfes quhen his Lot
May fumtyms four his Splein,
He rather fould mair lyke a Man,
Some braif Defign attempt;
Gif its nocht in his Pith, what than,
Reft but a Quhyle content,
Nocht feirful, but cheirful,
And wait the Will of Fate,
Which mynds to defygns to
Renew zour auntient State.

XII. I

XII.

I ken fum mair than ze do all
Of quhat fall afterwart befall,
    In mair aufpicious Tymes;
For aften far abufe the Mune,
We watching Beings do convene,
    Frae round Eards outmoft Climes,
Quhair evry Warden reprefents
    Cleirly his Nations Cafe,
Gif Famyne, Peft, or Sword Torments,
    Or Vilains hie in Place,
      Quha keip ay, and heip ay
      Up to themfelves grit Store,
      But rundging and fpunging
      The leil laborious Pure.

XIII.

Say then, faid I, at zour hie Sate,
Lernt ze ocht of auld *Scotlands* Fate,
    Gif eir fchoil be her fell;
With Smyle Celeft, quod he, I can,
But its nocht fit an mortal Man
    Sould ken all I can tell:

                  But

But Part to the I may unfold,
　　And thou may faifly ken,
Quhen *Scottiſh* Peirs flicht *Saxon* Gold,
　　And turn trew heartit Men;
　　　Quhen Knaivry and Slaivrie,
　　　Ar equally difpyfd,
　　　And Loyalte and Royalte,
　　　Univerfalie are pryfd.

XIV.

QUHEN all zour Trade is at a Stand,
And Cunzie clene forfaiks the Land,
　　Quhilk will be very fune,
Will Preifts without their Stypands preich,
For nocht will Lawyers Caufes Streich;
　　Faith thatis nae eafy done.
All this and mair maun cum to pafs,
　　To cleir zour glamourit Sicht;
And *Scotland* maun be made an Afs,
　　To fet her Jugment richt.
　　　Theyil jade hir and blad hir,
　　　Untill fcho brak hir Tether,
　　　Thocht auld fchois zit bauld fchois,
　　　And teuch lyke barkit Lether.

XV. BUT

XV.

But mony a Corfs fall braithlefs ly,
And Wae fall mony a Widow cry,
 Or all rin richt again;
Owre *Cheviot* prancing proudly *North*,
The Faes fall tak the Feild neir *Forthe*,
 And think the Day thair ain:
But Burns that Day fall rin with Blude
 Of them that now opprefs;
Thair Carcaffes be *Corbys* Fude,
 By thoufands on the Grefs.
 A King then fall ring them,
 Of wyfe Renoun and braif,
 Quhafe Pufians and Sapiens,
 Sall Richt reftoir and faif.

XVI.

The View of Freidomis fweit, quod I,
O fay, grit Tennant of the Skye,
 How neiris that happie Tyme.
We ken Things but be Circumftans,
Nae mair, quod he, I may advance,
 Leift I commit a Cryme.

Quhat

Quhat eir ze pleis, gae on, quod I,
    I fall not fafh ze moir,
Say how, and quhair ze met, and quhy,
    As ze did hint befoir.
        With Air then fae fair then,
        That glanft like Rayis of Glory,
        Sae Godlyk and oddlyk,
        He thus refumit his Storie.

XVII.

FRAE the Suns Ryfing to his Sett,
All the pryme Rait of Wardens met,
    In folemn bricht Array,
With Vehicles of *Aither* cleir,
Sic we put on quhen we appeir
    To Sauls rowit up in Clay;
Thair in a wyde and fplendit Hall,
    Reird up with fhynand Beims,
Quhais Rufe-treis wer of Rainbows all,
    And paift with ftarrie Gleims,
        Quhilk prinked and twinkled
        Brichtly beyont Compair,
        Much famed and named
        A Caftill in the Air.

XVIII. IN

XVIII.

In midft of quhilk a Tabill ftude,
A fpacious Oval reid as Blude,
 Made of a Fyre-Flaucht,
Arround the dazeling Walls were drawn,
With Rays be a celeftial Hand,
 Full mony a curious Draucht.
Inferiour Beings flew in Haift,
 Without Gyd or Derectour,
Millions of Myles throch the wyld Wafte,
 To bring in Bowlis of Nectar:
  Then roundly and foundly
  We drank lyk *Roman* Gods;
  Quhen *Jove* fae dois rove fae,
  That *Mars* and *Bacchus* nods.

XIX.

Quhen *Phebus* Heid turns licht as Cork,
And *Neptune* leans upon his Fork,
 And limpand *Vulcan* blethers:
Quhen *Pluto* glowrs as he were wyld,
And *Cupid* luves we wingit Chyld,
 Fals down and fyls his Fethers.

       Quhen

Quhen *Pan* forzets to tune his Reid,
　　And flings it cairlefs bye,
And *Hermes* wingd at Heils and Heid,
　　Can nowther ftand nor lye:
　　　　Quhen ftaggirand and fwagirrand,
　　　　They ftoyter Hame to fleip,
　　　　Quhyle Centeries at Enteries
　　　　Imortal Watches keip.

XX.

Thus we tuke in the high browin Liquour,
And bangd about the Nectar Biquour;
　　But evir with his Ods:
We neir in Drink our Judgments drenfch,
Nor fcour about to feik a Wenfch
　　Lyk thefe auld baudy Gods,
But franklie at ilk uther afk,
　　Quhats proper we fuld know,
How ilk ane hes performt the Tafk,
　　Affignd to him below.
　　　　Our Minds then fae kind then,
　　　　Are fixt upon our Care,
　　　　Ay noting and ploting
　　　　Quhat tends to thair Weilfair.

XXI. *Gothus*

XXI.

Gothus and *Vandall* baith lukt bluff,
Quhyle *Gallus* fneerd and tuke a Snuff,
  Quhilk made *Allmane* to ftare ;
Latinus bad him naithing feir,
But lend his Hand to haly Weir,
  And of cowd Crouns tak Care ;
Batavius with his Paddock-Face
  Luking afquint, cryd, Pifch,
Zour Monks ar void of Sence or Grace,
  I had leur ficht for Fifch ;
   Zour Schule-men ar Fule-men,
   Carvit out for dull Debates,
   Decoying and deftroying
   Baith Monarchies and States.

XXII.

Iberius with a gurlie Nod
Cryd, *Hogan*, zes we ken zour God,
  Its Herrings ze adore ;
Heptarchus, as he ufd to be,
Can nocht with his ain Thochts agre,
  But varies bak and fore ;

         Ane

Q

Ane quhyle he fays, It is not richt
　　A Monarch to refift,
Neift Braith all Ryall Powir will flicht,
　　And paffive Homage jeft;
　　　He hitches and fitches
　　　Betwein the *Hic* and *Hoc*,
　　　Ay jieand and flieand
　　　Round lyk a Wedder-cock.

XXIII.

1 ftill fupport my Precedens
Abune them all, for Sword and Sens,
　　Thocht I haif layn richt now lown,
Quhylk was, becaus I bure a Grudge
At fum fule *Scotis*, quha lykd to drudge
　　To Princes no thair awin;　　　·
Sum Thanis thair Tennants pykit and fqueift,
　　And purfit up all thair Rent,
Syne wallopit to far Courts, and bleift,
　　Till Riggs and Schaws war fpent;
　　　Syne byndging and whyndging,
　　　Quhen thus redufit to Howps,
　　　They dander and wander
　　　About pure Lickmadowps.

XXIV. But

XXIV.

BUT now its Tyme for me to draw
My fhynand Sword againft Club-Law,
  And gar my Lyon roir;
He fall or lang gie fic a Sound,
The Ecchoe fall be hard arround
  Europe, frae Schore to Schore;
Then lat them gadder all thair Strenth,
  And ftryve to wirk my Fall,
Tho numerous, zit at the lenth
  I will owrecum them all,
   And raife zit and blafe zit
   My Braifrie and Renown,
   By gracing and placing
   Arright the *Scottis* Crown.

XXV.

QUHEN my braif BRUCE the fame fall weir
Upon his Ryal Heid, full cleir
  The Diadem will fhyne;
Then fall zour fair Oppreffion ceis,
His Intreft zours he will not fleice,
  Or leif zou eir inclyne:

      Thocht

Thocht Millions to his Purſe be lent,
    Zell neir the puirer be,
But rather richer, quhyle its ſpent
    Within the *Scottiſh* Se:
        The Feild then ſall zeild then
        To honeſt Huſbands Welth,
        Gude Laws then ſall cauſe then
        A ſickly State haif Helth.

XXVI.

QUHYLE thus he talkit, methocht ther came
A wondir fair Etherial Dame,
    And to our Warden ſayd,
Grit *Callidon* I cum in Serch
Of zou, frae the hych ſtarry Arch,
    The Counſill wants zour Ayd;
Frae every Quarter of the Sky,
    As ſwift as Quhirl-wynd,
With Spirits ſpeid the Chiftains hy,
    Sum grit Thing is deſygnd
        Owre Muntains be Funtains,
        And round ilk fairy Ring,
        I haif chaiſt ze, O haiſt ze,
        They talk about zour King.

XXVII. WITH

XXVII.

Wɪᴛʜ that my Hand methocht he ſchuke,
And wiſcht I Happyneſs micht bruke,
　　To eild be Nicht and Dąy;
Syne quicker than an Arrows Flicht,
He mountit upwarts frae my Sicht,
　　Straicht to the milkie Way;
My Mynd him followit throw the Skyes,
　　Untill the brynie Streme
For Joy ran trinckling frae myne Eyes,
　　And wakit me frae Dreme;
　　　　Then peiping, half ſleiping,
　　　　Frae furth my rural Beild,
　　　　It eiſit me and pleiſit me
　　　　To ſe and ſmell the Feild.

XXVIII.

Fᴏʀ *Flora* in hir clene Array,
New waſhen with a Showir of *May*,
　　Lukit full ſweit and fair;
Quhyle hir cleir Huſband frae aboif
Sched doun his Rayis of genial Luve,
　　Hir Sweits perfumt the Air;

　　　　　　　　　　　The

The Winds war hufht, the Welkin cleird,
    The glumand Clouds war fled,
And all as faft and gay appeird
    As ane *Elyfion* Sched;
      Quhilk heifit and bleifit
      My Heart with fic a Fyre,
      As raifes thefe Praifes
      That do to Heaven afpyre.

              Quod AR. SCOT.

Jok Up-a-lands *Complaint againſt the Court in the Kings Nonaige.*

I.

NOw is the King in tendir Aige,
    O CHRYST! conſerve him in his Eild,
To do Juſtice to Man and Page,
    That gars our Land ly lang unteild,
Thocht we do double pay thair Wage;
    Pure Commons preſentlie ar peild.
They ryde about in ſic a Rege,
    Be Firth and Forreſt, Muir and Feild,
      With Bow Buckler and Brand.
    Lo quhair they ryde intill the Ry,
    The Deil mot ſane the Company,
    I pray it frae my Heart trewly:
      This ſaid *Jok Up-a-land.*

                    II. HE

II.

He that was wont to beir the Barrows,
  Betwixt the Bake-hous and the Brew-hous
On Twenty Shilling now he tarrows,
  To ryd the Heigait by the Plewis;
But were I King, and haif gude Fallows,
  In *Norroway* they fould heir of Newis,
I fould him tak, and all his Marrows,
  And hing them hich upon zon Hewis,
    And thairto plichts my Hand.
    And all thir Lordis and Barronis grit,
    Upon an Gallows fould I knit,
    That this doun treddit has our Quhit:
    This faid *Jok Up-a-land.*

III.

But wald ilk Lord that our Law leids,
  To Hufbands Reffone do with Skill,
To chak thir Chiftains be the Heids,
  And hing them heich upon ane Hill;
Then Hufbands labour micht their Steids,
  And Preifts micht pattir and pray their Fill:
For Hufbands fould nocht haif fic Pleids,
  And Scheip and Nolt micht ly full ftill,
    And Stakis and Rukis micht ftand;

For

For fen they raid amang our Dorrs,
With Splent on Spald and joufty Spurrs,
Thair grew nae Fruit intill our Furrs:
This faid *Jok Up-a-land.*

IV.

Tak a pure Man a Scheip or twae,
For Hungir or for Falt of Fude,
To five or fax wie Bairns or mae,
They will him hang in Halters rude;
But gif an tak a Flok or fae,
A Bow of Ky, and lat them blude,
Full faifly may he ryd or gae:
I wait nocht gif thir Laws be gude,
I fchrew them firft them fand.
O Jesu, for thy haly Paffioun,
Grant to him Grace that weirs the Crown,
To ding thir mony Kings all doun:
This faid *Jok Up-a-land.*

Quod KENNEDY.

THE

THE
Garment of gude LADYIS.

I.

WALD my gude Lady lufe me beſt,
 And work aftir my Will,
I ſould a Garment gudlieſt,
 Gar mak hir Body till.

II.

OF Honour hie ſould be hir Hude,
 Upon hir Heid to weir,
Garniſt with Governance ſae gude,
 Nae demyeng ſould hir deir.

III.

HIR Sark ſould be, hir Body nixt,
 Of Chaſtitie ſae quhyte,
With Schame and Dreid togither mixt,
 The ſame ſould be perfyt.

IV. HIR

IV.

Hɪʀ Kirtle of the clene Conſtance,
  Doun laiſt with leſum Luve;
The Melzies of Continuance,
  For nevir to remuve.

V.

Hɪʀ Goun ſould be of Gudlienes,
  Weil Riband with Renown,
Purfillt with Pleſour in ilk Place,
  And furt with fyne Faſſoun.

VI.

Hɪʀ Belt ſould be of Benignitie,
  About hir Midil meit,
Hir Mantil of Humilitie,
  To tholl baith Wind and Weit.

VII.

Hɪʀ Hat ſould be of fair Having,
  Hir Tipat of the Truth;
Hir Paitlet of ay gude pauſing,
  Hir Hals Riban of Rewth.

VIII. Hɪʀ

VIII.

HɪR Sleives fould be of Efperance,
  To keip hir frae Difpair;
Hir Gluves of the beft Governance,
  To hyd hir Fingers fair.

IX.

HɪR Shune fould be of Sickernefs,
  In Time that fcho nocht flyd;
Hir Hofe of Honefty exprefs,
  I fould for hir provyde.

X.

WALD fcho put on this Garment gay,
  I durft fweir be my Seill,
That fcho wore nevir Grene nor Gray,
  That fet hir half fo weil.

Quod Mr. ROB. HENRYSON.

To the Honour of the Ladyis, and the Fortification of their Fame.

I.

JUST to declair the hie Magnificence,
    And Bountie grit that in the Ladyis is,
The Wirdynefs and Verteus Excelence,
    The Laud, the Truth, the Bewtie, and the Blifs,
    My Barbir Tung unworthy is I wifs;
But nocht the lefs my Pen I will apply,
    To fay the Suth, thoch Eloquence I mifs,
Of Femenyne the Fame to fortify.

II.

THOCHT Doctors auld Addreffes thair Delyt,
    To dyt of Ladys Defamation,
Wae worth the Wicht fould fet his Appityte,
    To reid fic Rolls of Reprobation;
    But tittar mak plain Proclamation,
To gather all fic Lybills biffelie,
    And in the Fyre mak thair Location,
Of Femenyne the Fame to fortifie.

III. FOR

III.

For quho fae lift the Richt trew to reherfe,
    To humane Glore they mak Habilitie;
Quhen Men ar fad at them folace they ferfs,
    As Habitickles of all Humanity,
    They bring grit Weirs aft to Tranquilitie,
Malice of Men they meis and pacifie,
    To Saul and Body baith Utilitie;
Therfore all Men thair Fame fould fortifie.

IV.

Althocht a Man had as much Gude to fpend
    As all the Empyres of this Globe around;
Wer Women wanting Weil-fare were at End,
    Without thair Comfort Care fould him confound;
    Quhair they abyde thair Blifs does ay abound,
And quhair they flie Felicetie gaes by;
    Bot thair Solace nae Sage may be eir found;
Thairfore all Men thair Fame fould fortifie.

V.

Sen GOD has grantit them fic Gudlinefs,
    And formid them after fae fyne faffoun,
Syne put fic bluming Bewtie in thair Face,
    Quhy fould not Men hald them of grit Renown?
                          Sen

Sen God has given to them fae grit Guerdoun,
And with fic Meiknes does them magnifie,
  Quhy fould Men mak to them Comparifone,
But owre all quhair thair Fames to fortifie?

VI.

Of *Mary* myld, the Maid imaculate,
  To fortifie of Femenyne the Fame,
Chryst was incarnate and incorporate,
  And nurift was nyn Months within hir Wame;
  And aftir born, and bocht us frae the Blame
Of *Bellial*, that brint us bitterlie;
  That heavenly Honour faves the Sex frae Shame,
And owre all quhair thair Fame dois fortifie.

               Quod STEWART.

THE

THE

DAUNCE.

I.

OF *Februar* the fiftein Nicht,
　　Richt lang before the Dayis Licht,
　　　　I lay intill a Trance,
And then I faw baith Heaven and Hell,
Methocht amang the Feynds fell
　　Mahoun gart cry a Daunce,
Of Shrewis that wer nevir fchrevin
Againft the Feift of Fafterns Evin,
　　　　To mak thair Obfervance;
He bad Galands gae graith a Gyis,
And caft up Gamonds to the Skyes,
　　　　That laft came out of *France.*

II. Let

II.

Let fee, quod he, now quha begins:
With that the foull feven deadly Sins
 Begouth to leip attains;
And firft of all the Daunce was *Pryde*,
With Hair wyld back, Bonnet on Syde,
 Lyk to mak vaiftie Wains;
And round about him as a Quheil,
Hang all in Rumples to his Heil
 His Kethat for the Nains:
Mony proud Trumpour with him trippit
Throw fkaldan Fyre, ay as they fkipit
 They girnd with hydious Granes.

III.

Hellie Harlots on hawtane Ways
Came in with mony findry Gyis,
 Zit nevir leuch *Mahoun*,
Till Preifts came with bare fchaven Necks,
Then all the Feynds leuch and made Gecks,
 Black-wame and Bawfy-broun.

IV. Then

R

IV.

THEN *Yre* came in with Sturt and Stryfe,
His Hand was ay upon his Knyfe,
 He brandeiſt lyk a Beir:
Boaſters, Braggers and Barganers
Aftir him paſsd all in be Pairs,
 All boddin in Feir of Weir;
In Jacks, Stripps, and Bonnets of Steil,
Thair Leggs wer chenziet to the Heil,
 Frawart was thair Affeir;
With Brands ſum on uther beft,
Sum jagit uthers to the Heft
 With Knives that Scheip coud ſcheir.

V.

NEXT followd in the Daunce, *Envy,*
Filld full of Feid and Fellony,
 Hid Malyce and Diſpyt;
For privy Hate that Traytor trembled,
Him followd mony Freik, diſſembled
 With fenzied Words quhyte,

And

And Flatterers into Mens Faces,
And Back-byters of ſundry Races,
 To lie that had Delyte,
With Rownars vyle of falſe Leiſings;
Allace! that Courts of nobil Kings
 Of ſic can neer be quyte.

VI.

NIXT him in Daunce came *Covetyce,*
Rute of all Ill, and Grund of Vyce,
 That neir could be content;
Catyvs, Wretches and Ockerars,
Hud Pykes, Hurders and Gatherers,
 All with that *Warlo* went:
Out of thair Throts they ſhot on uther,
Het moltin Gold methocht a Futher,
 As Fyre-flaucht maiſt fervent;
Ay as they tuimt themſells of Schot,
Feynds filld them weil up to the Throt
 With Gold of all kynd Prent.

VII.

SYNE *Sweirnes* at the ſecond Bidding
Came lyk a Sow out of a Midding,
 Full ſleipy was his Grunzie;

Mony

Mony fweir bumbard Belly-huddron,
Mony Slut, Daw, and fleipy Duddron,
 Him ferved ay with Sounzie:
He drew them furth intill a Chenzie,
And *Belial* with a Bridall Renzie
 Ay lafhit them on the Lunzie.
In Daunce they wer fae flaw of Feit,
They gaif them in the Fyre a Heit,
 Made them quicker of Cunzie.

VIII.

THEN *Lechery*, that laithly Corfs,
Berand lyk to a bagit Horfs,
 And Ydlenefs did him leid;
Ther was with him ane ugly Sort,
And mony a ftynkand foull Tramort
 That had in Sin bene deid:
Quhen they wer enterit in the Daunce,
They wer full ftrange of Countenance,
 Lyk *Turkas* burnand reid;
All led they uther by the ——
Suppofe they fyket with thair ——
 It micht be nae Remeid.

       IX. THEN

IX.

THEN the foull Monſter, *Gluttony*,
With Wame unſatiate and greidy,
    To daunce ſyn did him dreſs;
Him followit mony a foull Drunkart
With Can and Colep, Cop and Quart,
    In Surfet and Exceſs;
Full mony a waiſtleſs wally Drag,
With Wames unwyldy did forth wag
    In Creiſh, that did increſs;
Drink, ay they cryd, with mony a Gaip,
The Feynds gave them het Lead to laip,
    Thair Lovery was nae leſs.

X.

NAE Minſtralls playd to them bot Dout,
For Glie-men ther war haldin out
    Be Day and eik by Nicht;
Except a Minſtrall that ſlew a Man,
Sae till his Heritage he wan,
    Entert be Breif of Richt.

XI. THEN

XI.

Then cryd *Mahoun* for a *Earſe* Padzean,
Syn ran a Feynd to fetch *Makfadzean*,
　　Far Northwart in a Nuke;
Be he the Correnoch did ſchout,
Earſe Men ſo gatherit him about,
　　In Hell grit Rume they tuke:
That Tarmagants with Tag and Tatter,
Full loud in *Earſe* begoud to clatter
　　And rowp lyk Ravin and Rowk;
The Deil ſae deivt was with thair Yell,
That in the deipeſt Pot of Hell
　　He ſmorit them all with Smuke.

Follows the Tournament between the Soutar and Tailzior.

I.

NIxt that a Tournament was cryd,
 That lang before in Hell was tryd,
  In Prefence of *Mahoun*,
Betwifch a Tailzior and a Soutar,
A Prick-Loufe and a Hobell-Clouter,
  The Barrefs was made boun;
The Tailzior baith with Speir and Sheild,
Convoyit was into the Feild,
  With mony a Lymmar-Loun,
Of Seme-byters and Beift-knappers,
Of Stomok-ftealers and Claith-takers,
  A graceles Garrifoun.

II. His

II.

His Banner was born him before,
Quherin was Clouts a hundred Score,
 Ilk ane of diverſe Heu,
And all ſtown out of ſindry Webs,
For quhyle the *Greik* Se flows and ebs,
 Tailziors will neir be trew:
The Tailzior on the Barrows blent,
Allace! he tint all Hardyment,
 For Feir he changit Hew:
Mahoun came forth and maid him Knicht,
Nae Ferlie thocht his Heart was licht,
 That to ſic Honour grew.

III.

The Tailzior hecht before *Mahoun*,
That he ſuld ding the Soutar doun,
 Wer he ſtrang as a Maſt;
But quhen he on the Barrous blenkit,
His clouted Courage fairly ſchrinkit,
 His Heart did all owre-caſt:

Quhen

Quhen to the Soutar he did cum,
Of all fic Words he was quyte dum,
　　Sae fair he was agaſt.
In Heart he tuke fae great a Scunder,
A Rak of Farts lyke ony Thunder,
　　Flew frae him Blaſt for Blaſt.

IV.

THE Soutar to the Feild him dreſt,
He was convoyid out of the Weſt,
　　As an Deffender ſtout.
Suppofe he had nae luſty Varlet,
He had full mony a loufy Harlot,
　　Round ryding him about.
His Banner was of barkit Hyd,
Quherin Saint *Girnega* did glyd,
　　Before that Rebald Rout:
Full Soutar lyke he was of Laits;
For ay betwifh his Harnes Plaits,
　　The Uly burſtit out.

V.

QUHEN on the Tailzior he did luke,
His Heart a litle Dwaming tuke,
　　He micht not richt upfit,

Into

Into his Stommok was ſic a Steir,
Of all his Denner quhilk he coft deir,
   His Breaſt held Deil a Bit:
To comfort him or he raid furder,
The Deil of Knichthude gaif him Order,
   Fou ſair ſyne did he ſpit;
And he about the Devils Neck,
Did ſpew again a Quart of Blek,
   Thus knichtly he him quit.

VI.

Then Fourty Times the Feynd cryd, Fy,
The Soutar richt afearedly,
   Unto the Feild he ſocht:
Quhen they were ſerved with their Speirs,
Folk had a Feil be their Effeirs,
   Their Hearts were baith on Flocht,
They ſpurd their Horſs on either Syde,
Syne they outowre the Grund coud glyd,
   And them togither brocht.
The Tailzior that was nocht weil ſitten,
He left his Sadle all beſhitten,
   And to the Grund he ſocht.

VII. His

VII.

His Harnes brak and made a Brattle,
The Soutars Horſs lap with a Ratle,
   And round about coud reil:
The Beiſt that frayed was richt evil,
Ran with the Soutar to the Devil,
   Him he rewardit weil:
Sumthing frae him the Feynd eſhewd,
He wont again to bein beſpewd,
   So ſtern he was in Steil:
He thocht again he wald debate him,
He turnd his Erſe, and all bedret him,
   Ein quyte frae Neck to Heil.

VIII.

He lowſit it aff with ſic a Reird;
He dang baith Horſs and Man till Eard,
   He fartit with ſic Feir.
Now haif I quit thee, quoth *Mahoun*,
Thir new made Knichts lay baith in Swoun,
   And did all Arms menſweir;

The

The Deil gart them to Dungeon dryve,
And them of Knichthude could depryve,
　　Difcharging them of Weir,
And made them Harlots baith for evir,
Quhilk ftill to keip they had far levir
　　Nor ony Arms to beir.

IX.

I had mair of their Warks written,
Had not the Soutar bein befhitten,
　　With *Belials* Erfs unblift.
But that fae gude a Bourd methocht,
Sic Solace to my Heart it brocht,
　　For Lauchter neir I brift:
Quherthrow I wakenit frae my Trance,
To put this in Rememberance,
　　Micht no Man me refift;
For this faid Jufting it befell,
Befoir *Mahoun* the Air of Hell,
　　Now trew this gif ze lift.

Here ends the Soutar and the Tailziors War,
Made be the noble Poet W^m. Dunbar.

Follows

Follows ane

Amends made to the forefaid
Knichts of the Birs and Thumble;
In Cafe his Joke fhould them provok
Owr fair to girn and grumble.

I.

BEtwisht the Twelt Hour and Elevin,
 I dreamd an Angel came frae Heavin,
With Pleafand Stevin fayand on hie,
Tailziors and Soutars bliſt be ze.

II.

HIGH up for zou is ordaind a Place,
Abune all Saints in great Solace,
In Happyneſs and Dignity,
Tailziors and Soutars bliſt be ze.

III. THE

III.

THE Caufe to you is not unkend,
Natures Negleft ye do amend,
Be Craft and great Agility,
Tailziors and Soutars blift be ze.

IV.

SOUTARS with Schune weil made and meit,
Ze mend the Faults of illfard Feit,
Quherfore to Heavin zour Sauls will flie,
Soutars and Tailziors blift be ze.

V.

THERIS not in this Fair a Flyrock,
That has upon his Feit a Wyrock,
Knoul Taes, or Mouls in nae Degre,
But ze can hyde them, blift be ze.

VI.

AND Tailziors ze with weil made Clais,
Can mend the warft made Man that gaes,
And mak him feimly lyk to fee,
Tailziors and Soutars blift be ze.

VII. THOCHT

VII.

THOCHT ane fuld haif a broken Back,
Haif he a Tailzior gude, quhat-rak,
Heill cover it richt craftely,
Tailziors and Soutars blift be ze.

VIII.

OF all great Kindes may ze claim,
The cruke Backs, and the Criple, Lame,
Ay howdrand Faults with zour fuplie,
Tailziors and Soutars blift be ze.

IX.

IN Eard ze kyth fic Ferlys heir,
In Heavin ze fall be Saints full cleir,
Tho ze be Knaves in this Countrie.
Soutars and Tailziors blift be ze.

Quod DUNBAR.

The

The Luvers Mane that dares not aſſay.

I.

QUHEN *Flora* had owrfrett the Firth,
  In *May* of ilka Moneth Quene,
Quhen Merle and Mavis ſings with Mirth,
  Sweit Melling in the Schaws ſae ſchene,
  When Luvers all rejoſit bene,
And maiſt diſyrous of thair Prey,
  I hard a luſty Luver mene,
I luve, but I dare not aſſay !

II.

STRANG ar the Pains I daylie pruve,
  But zit with Patience I ſuſtene,
I am ſae fettert in the Luve,
  Only of my ſweit Lady ſchene,
  Quhilk for her Bewtie micht be Quene,
Nature ſae craftily alway,
  Has done depaint that ſweit Serene,
Quhom I luve, and dare not aſſay.

III. SCHO

III.

Scho is fae bricht of Hyd and Hew,
 I luve but hir allone I wene,
Is nane hir Luve that may efchew,
  That blenks fae of that dulce Amene;
  Sae comelie cleir ar hir twa Ene,
That fcho mae Luvers does effrey,
  Then eir of *Greice* did fair *Helene*,
Quhome I luve, and dar not affay.

      Quod STEWART.

             Ane

Ane litle Interlude of the Droichs.

I.

Hirry, hary, hobbilſchow,
    Se ze not quha is cum now,
But zit wate I nevir how,
    Brocht with the Quhirl-wind;
A Sargeand out of *Soudoun* Land,
A Gyane ſtrang in Limbs to ſtand,
That with the Strength of my awin Hand
    May Bairs and Bugles bind.

II.

Quha is then cum heir, but I
A bauld and bowſteous Bellomy,
Amang zou all to cry a Cry
    With a maiſt michty Soun?
I generit am of Gyans kynd,
Frae hardy *Hercules* be Strynd,
Of all the Occident and Ynd,
    My Elders woir the Croun.

III. My

III.

My fore Grandfyre heicht *Fynmackoull*,
Quha dang the Deil, and gart him zoul,
The Skyes raind Fludes quhen he wald fkoul,
 He trublit all the Air.
He gat my Gudfyre *Gog Magog*,
He, when he daunft, the Warld wald fchog,
Then Thoufand Ells zied in his Frog
 Of Highland Plaids, and mair.

IV.

Sic was he quhen of tendir Zouth,
But aftir he grew mair at Fouth,
Elevin Myle wyde mett was his Mouth,
 His Teith was ten Myles fquair:
He wald upon his Tais upftand,
And tak the Starns doun with his Hand,
And fet them in a Gold Garland,
 Abuve his Wyfes Hair.

V.

His Wyfe fcho mekle was of Clift,
Her Heid wan heicher than the Lift,
The Hevin reirdit quhen fcho did rift,
 The Lafs was naithing fklender:

       Scho

Scho ſpat *Loch-lowmond* with hir Lips,
Thunder and Fyre flew frae hir Hips,
Quhen ſcho was crabbit, the Sun thold Clips ;
    The Feynd durſt nocht offend hir.

VI.

FOR Cauld ſcho tuke the Fever Tartane,
For all the Claith in *France* and *Bartane*
Wald not be to hir Leg a Gartane,
    Thocht ſcho was zung and tendir :
Upon a Nicht heir in the North,
Scho tuke the Gravel, and ſtaild *Craig-gorth*,
And piſcht the grit Watter of *Forth*,
    Sic Tyd ran aftirhind hir.

VII.

ANE Thing written of hir I find,
In *Yrland* quhen ſcho blew behind,
On *Norway* Coiſt ſcho raiſt the Wind,
    And grit Schips drownit thair :
Then ſcho fiſcht all the *Spainzie* Seis,
With hir Sark Lap betwix hir Theyis,
And thre Days ſailing tween hir Kneis
    It was eſteemd and mair.
              VIII. THE

VIII.

THE hingan Braes on Adir Syde
Scho powtert with hir Lymms fae wyde;
Laffes micht lair at hir to ftryde,
    Wald gae to Luvairs lair.
Scho markit to the Land with Mirth,
Scho quhirrd fyve Quhails into the Firth,
Had croppin on hir *Geig for Girth,
    Walterand amang the Wair.

IX.

MY Fader mekle *Gow Macmorne,*
Out of his Moders Wame was fchorne,
For Littlenes fcho was forlorn,
    Sican a Kemp to beir :
Or he of Age was Zeirs thre,
Hc wald ftap owre the Ocean Se,
The Mone fprang neir abune his Knie,
    The Heavens had of him Feir.

                  X. ANE

---

* A Kind of an old fafhioned Net ufed now for catching of
Spouts.

X.

ANE thoufand Ziers ar paft frae Mynd,
Sen I was generit of his Kynd,
Far furth in Defarts of the Ynd,
    Amang Lyon and Beir:
Worthy King *Arthur* and *Gawane,*
And mony a bauld Bairn of *Bartane*
Ar deid, and in the Wars are flain,
    Sen I could weild a Speir.

XI.

THE *Sophie* and the *Sowdoun* ftrang,
With Battles that haif laftit lang,
Out of thair Bounds has maid me gang,
    And turn to *Turkie* tyte.
The King of *Francis* grit Armie
Has brocht a Derth in *Lombardie,*
That in the Countrie I and he
    Can nocht dwell baith perfyte.

XII.

Swadrick, Danmark, and *Noraway,*
Nor in the Steids I dar not gae,
For ther is nocht but burn and flae,
    Cut Thropples and mak quyte.

                                             Yrland

Yrland for ay L haif refufit,
All wyfe Men will hald me excufit;
For neir in Land wher *Earfe* is ufit,
  To dwell had I delyt.

XIII.

I haif bene foremoft ay in Feild,
And now fae lang haif born the Scheild,
That I am crynit in for Eild
  This litle, as ze may fe:
I haif bene banift undir the Lynd
This lang Tyme, that nane could me fynd,
Quhyle now with this laft Eiftin Wynd,
  I am cum heir perdie.

XIV.

My Name is *Welth*, therfore be blyth,
I am cum Comfort zou to kyth,
Suppofe ilk Wretch fuld wail and wryth,
  All Derth I fall gar die:
For certainly the Truth to tell,
I cum amang ze now to dwell,
Far frae the Sound of *Curphour* Bell,
  To live I neir fall drie.
       XV. Now

XV.

Now fen I am fic Quantitie
Of Gyans cum, as ze may fe,
Quhair will be gotten a Wyfe for me,
    Of ficlyk Breid and Hicht?
In all this Bour is not a Bryde
Ane Hour I wate dar me abyde,
Zet trow ze ony Heir befyde
    Micht fuffer me all Nicht.

XVI.

ADEW a quhyle, for now I gae,
But I will not lang byde ze frae,
I wifch ze be conferft from Wae,
    Baith Maiden, Wyfe and Man:
GOD blefs them and the haly Rude,
Gif me a Drink, fe it be gude,
And quha trows beft that I do lude,
    Skink firft to me the Kan.

        FINIS. The Droichs Part of a Play.

Auld

Auld Kyndnefs quite forzet quhen ane grows pure.

I.

THis Warld is all but fenziet fair,
  And as unftable as the Wind,
And Faith is flemit I wat not quhair,
  Treft Fallowfhip is ill to find,
  Gude Confciences is all made blind,
And Charity thairs nane to get;
  Leil Luve and Lawty lys behind,
And auld Kyndnefs is quite forzet.

II.

QUHYLE I had ony Thing to fpend,
  And ftuffit weil with Warlds Wrack,
Amang my Friends I was weil kend;
  Quhen I was proud and had a Pack,
  They wad me be the Oxter tak;
And at the hich Buird I was fet,
  But now they let me ftand aback,
Sen auld Kyndnefs is quite forzet.

III. Now

III.

Now I can find but Friends few,
  Sen I was prized to be pure,
They hald me now but for a Shrew;
  Of me they tak but little Cure;
  All that I do is but Injure:
Thocht I be bair I may not bett,
  They let me ſtand upon the Flure,
Sen auld Kyndneſs is quite forzet.

IV.

Suppose I mein I am nocht mendit,
  Sen I held part with Povertie,
Away ſen that my Pack was ſpendit,
  Adieu all Liberality.
  The Proverb now is trew I ſee,
Quha may not give will little get;
  Therefore to ſay the Verity,
Now auld Kyndneſs is quite forzet.

V.

They wald me hals with Hude and Hat,
  Quhyle I was rich and had enouch,
About me Friends enow I gat;
  Richt blythly then on me they leuch,
  But now they mak it wonder teuch,
And lets me ſtand before the Zet;
  Therfoir this Warld is very freuch,
And auld Kyndneſs is quite forzet.　　VI. As

VI.

As lang as my ain Cap ftude even,
  I zied but feindle myne allane,
I fquyrit was with Sax or Sevin,
  Ay quhyle I gave them twa for ane;
  But fuddenly frae that was gane,
They pafsd me by with Hands plett,
  With puirtith frae I was oertane,
Then auld Kyndnefs was quite forzet.

VII.

INTO this Warld fuld nae Man trow,
  Thou may weil fee the Reafon quhy;
For ay but gif thy Hand be fou,
  Thou art but little fetten by,
  Thou art not tane in Company,
Bot ther be fund Fifh in thy Net:
  Therfore this falfe Warld I defy,
Sen auld Kyndnefs is quite forzet.

VIII.

SEN that nae Kyndnefs kepit is,
  Into this Warld that is prefent,
Gif thou wald cum to Heavins Blifs,
  Thyfelf appleift with fober Rent,
  Live weil and give with gude Intent,
To every Man his proper Debt,
  Quhat eir God fend hald thee content,
Sen auld Kyndnefs is quite forzet.　*AD-*

ADVICE to be Liberal and Blyth.

I.

I MAKE it kend, he that will ſpend,
　And luve GOD late and Air,
He will him mend, and Grace him ſend,
　Quhyle Catives ſhall have Care:
But Praiſe weil pend, ſall him comend,
　That of his Rowth can ſpare;
We knaw the End, that all maun wend
　Away nakit and bare,
With an O and an I,
　And a Wretch ſall haif nae mair,
But a ſchort Sheit at Heid and Feit,
　For all his Wrak and Ware.

II. FOR

II.

For all the Wrak a Wretch can pack,
  And in his Bags embrace,
Zit Deid fall tak him be the Back,
  And gar him cry Alace!
Then fall he fwak, away with Lak,
  And wate not to what Place,
Then will they mak, at him a Knack,
  That maift of his Geir hes;
With ane O and an I,
  Quhyle we haif Tyme and Space,
Mak we gude Cheir, quhyle we are heir,
  And thankful be for Grace.

III.

Were there a King to rax and ring,
  Amang Gude-fallows crownd,
Wretches wad wring, and mak Murning,
  For Dule they fould be drownd.
Quha finds a Dring, or auld or zing,
  Gar hoy him out and hound.

Now

Now let us fing, our Cares to ding,
　　And mak a gladfome Sound,
With an O and ane I:
　　Now are we further bound,
Drink thou to me, and I to thee,
　　And let the Cap go round.

IV.

QUHA underftude, fuld have his Gude,
　　Or he were clofd in Clay,
Sum in thair Mude they wald ga wid,
　　And die lang or thair Day;
Not worth a Hude, or an auld Snude
　　Thou fhall bear hence away;
Wretch be the Rude, now to conclude,
　　Full few fall for thee pray,
With an O and ane I,
　　Gude Fallows as langs we may,
Be merry and free, fyne blyth let us be,
　　And fing on tway and tway.

Quod Jo. BLYTH.

The End of the firft Volume.

CONTENTS

OF THE

Firſt VOLUME.

www.ingramcontent.com/pod-product-compliance
Lightning Source LLC
Chambersburg PA
CBHW030625030726
47497CB00006B/1635